Portland Midwives

From rivalry to romance!

Dedicated midwives and best friends Hazel and
Bria cofounded and run the Multnomah Falls
Women's Health Center in Portland, Oregon.
Their holistic approach brings moms-to-be from
far and wide. But they're ruffling a couple of
feathers over at the local St. Raymond's Hospital…

That is, before all that friction turns into
flirtation…and these two midwives discover that
the miracle of love is just as powerful as
the miracle of life!

Read Hazel's story in
The Doctor She Should Resist
by Amy Ruttan

Discover Bria's story in
The Midwife from His Past
by Julie Danvers

Both available now!

Dear Reader,

I'm thrilled to present you with this installment of the Portland Midwives duet. I immediately entered fangirl mode when I learned I'd be writing a story in a shared setting with Amy Ruttan. We decided to write a story about midwives with themes from our favorite Jane Austen novels—*Pride and Prejudice* in her case, and *Persuasion* in mine.

I thought paying homage to one of my favorite books would make writing easier, but it turns out that what works in the eighteenth century doesn't translate seamlessly to the twenty-first. Fortunately, I'm not one to back away from a challenge, and neither is my heroine, Bria Thomas.

Bria was heartbroken years ago when family pressure ruined her chance at love. She's worked hard to rebuild her life. But when smoldering Eliot Wright returns to Portland, he upends the careful balance she's crafted for herself. Both of them know it would be a bad idea to act on the attraction they feel for one another. But sometimes bad ideas are the most difficult to resist.

Life has offered Bria and Eliot a second chance. Whether it lasts forever is up to them!

Hope you enjoy!

Julie Danvers

JulieDanvers.WordPress.com

THE MIDWIFE
FROM HIS PAST

JULIE DANVERS

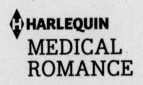

HARLEQUIN®
MEDICAL
ROMANCE™

Recycling programs
for this product may
not exist in your area.

ISBN-13: 978-1-335-40932-4

The Midwife from His Past

Copyright © 2022 by Alexis Silas

All rights reserved. No part of this book may be used or reproduced in
any manner whatsoever without written permission except in the case of
brief quotations embodied in critical articles and reviews.

This is a work of fiction. Names, characters, places and incidents
are either the product of the author's imagination or are used fictitiously.
Any resemblance to actual persons, living or dead, businesses,
companies, events or locales is entirely coincidental.

For questions and comments about the quality of this book,
please contact us at CustomerService@Harlequin.com.

Harlequin Enterprises ULC
22 Adelaide St. West, 41st Floor
Toronto, Ontario M5H 4E3, Canada
www.Harlequin.com

Printed in U.S.A.

Julie Danvers grew up in a rural community surrounded by farmland. Although her town was small, it offered plenty of scope for imagination, as well as an excellent library. Books allowed Julie to have many adventures from her own home, and her love affair with reading has never ended. She loves to write about heroes and heroines who are adventurous, passionate about a cause, and looking for the best in themselves and others. Julie's website is juliedanvers.wordpress.com.

Books by Julie Danvers

Harlequin Medical Romance

From Hawaii to Forever
Falling Again in El Salvador
Secret from Their LA Night

Visit the Author Profile page at Harlequin.com.

For Karlynn, who got those quintuplets out safely.

**Praise for
Julie Danvers**

"Julie Danvers, a newish author to HQN Medical Romances, is now one of my favorites. She's masterful at adding tiny, authentic details that pull you into an exotic setting."

—*Goodreads*

CHAPTER ONE

BRIA THOMAS HAD spotted an impostor.

She and her best friend, Hazel Rees, strolled along the bank of Willamette River, both with a coffee in hand. Portland's weekly open-air market bustled around them, the voices of hagglers mingling in the early fall air with the strains of music from street performers.

"There," Bria said, gesturing with her coffee-laden hand. "That woman with the tan coat. She's definitely a spy."

"Are you sure?" asked Hazel. "She seems pretty ordinary to me."

"That's exactly what a spy would want you to think. She may look plain on the outside, but that handbag of hers probably holds all kinds of State Department secrets."

There was nothing Bria loved more than getting coffee with Hazel and going to Portland's Saturday Market. Like Bria, Hazel was a mid-wife, although her friend was a nurse practitioner, too, and the two of them were cofounders of the Multnomah Falls Women's Health Center. Pulling double duty as midwives and starting up a nonprofit organization had kept them extremely busy, but now that it was up and running, spending Saturday morning together had come to be a fiercely protected tradition, no matter how much work they had to do. The two of them would spend hours concocting elaborate backstories for people in the crowd. The human statue performing on the corner was actually in the witness protection program, hiding from the Mob in plain sight. The cyclist pausing for a drink on the sidewalk was a world-class athlete, training for glory after tragically losing everything years ago.

The spy moved on to another booth, examining various pieces of jewelry crafted by local artists.

"Hmm. Perhaps you're right," Hazel agreed, taking a sip of her coffee. "Ooh! Secret billionaire to the left." She nodded toward a man in a large hat and cowboy boots.

"*Secret* billionaire? How can you tell?"

Hazel laughed. "Bria Thomas. You, of all people, should know a secret billionaire when you see one."

"I guess I've lost my touch." Bria moved to tuck her hair behind her ears, an old habit from before she'd gotten the pixie cut that now framed her large green eyes. She didn't miss the dark waves that had once fallen around her shoulders—she'd always been petite, and all that hair had only made her look shorter. But she occasionally forgot that it wasn't there anymore. She'd been through so many changes over the past few years that sometimes it was hard to keep up with them.

Once, Bria might have been as skilled at picking the well-bred and wealthy out of a crowd as she was at spotting a real Prada handbag from a mountain of designer knockoffs. Her family was one of the oldest and wealthiest in Portland. But taking her family's money had also meant accepting being under their control. She'd stepped down from her family's trust years ago, deciding that she preferred independence to living in a gilded cage. Her life was drastically different than it used to be, back when her idea of a relaxing Saturday morning involved a trip to the Maldives by private jet, or a few days at an exclusive spa. But it was her life, and while it might not be glamorous, she was proud of what she'd been able to accomplish. She loved her career as a midwife, and she had good friends like Hazel in her life. And as far as her love life was concerned…well, she supposed one couldn't have everything.

Dating had never been easy for her. It had been years since she'd had anyone serious in her life. Part of that was because of her work. Up until last year, she'd spent two years working for an international aid organization in Haiti. There hadn't been many dating opportunities while working abroad, and she'd preferred it that way. In her experience, dating led to misunderstandings, hurt feelings and heartbreak, and she'd wanted to focus on her career without the complications that accompanied romance.

But she also wanted to have a family someday. She knew, of course, that it was possible to have a child on her own, but she'd always dreamed of having a family built on the love between herself and someone else. The trouble was, her attempts to find that someone else ranged from bad to completely disastrous.

When she'd returned from Haiti last year, she'd tried to ease herself back into the dating scene. But thus far, her attempts at dating had only led to a string of awful romantic encounters. There'd been the man she'd met online who turned out to be married—fortunately she'd found out after just a few weeks. Another man claimed to be looking for a long-term relationship, but he really just wanted to use Bria as his cat sitter whenever he went out of town, which seemed to be every single weekend. Another had texted frequently but canceled at the last minute every time they'd made plans to meet in person.

Frustrated and discouraged, she'd decided to take a break from dating. But that hadn't stopped Hazel from trying to nudge her toward men whenever possible. At the moment, Hazel seemed to have set her sights on one target in particular.

"I'm telling you, Bria, he's a secret billionaire. He probably thinks he's fooling everyone by walking around in those dusty, worn-out jeans—which are quite flattering to the figure, I must say—but the quality of the boots gives him away. And I don't see a wedding ring." She raised her eyebrows meaningfully at Bria.

Bria shook her head. "Nice try. With my luck, Mr. Secret Billionaire over there would probably turn out to be Mr. Secret Serial Killer." She knew that Hazel meant well, but she also thought that Hazel tended to think about relationships through the biased lens of her own success. Hazel had found her own happiness with Dr. Caleb Norris, who until recently had been chief of obstetrics at St. Raymond's, the birthing hospital across from the Women's Health Center. Bria knew that Hazel simply wanted her to find as much happiness as she had. But Bria was starting to doubt that she'd ever have a real chance at love. Her attempts at relationships had at best led to awkwardness and discomfort…and at worst, life-shattering heart-break. She'd been through that kind of heart-break once in her life, and she had no desire to repeat the experience.

"How's Caleb feeling about leaving St. Ray-mond's now that he's finished working out his notice?" she asked Hazel, hoping to change the subject. "Have they found a replacement for him yet?" Caleb had quit his job at the hospital so he could set up his own private practice at the Women's Health Center as an obstetrician, as he'd developed a desire to do more holistic work with patients. Bria was excited to have a physi-cian of Caleb's ability available to them, as that would only help the center's reputation grow. Normally, Hazel's eyes brightened whenever the subject of Caleb came up. But Bria was sur-prised to see Hazel's brow tighten with worry.

"Hazel? Is something wrong?"

"Look… I need to tell you something. And there's no easy way to say it."

Bria instantly felt guilty. Here she was obsess-ing over her own problems with love and dat-ing when Hazel needed to talk about something. "What is it? The center didn't lose more money, did it?" Although the Multnomah Falls Wom-en's Health Center was wildly popular among patients, many of their clients couldn't afford to pay for the entire cost of their care, and the center was dependent on grants and donations. Recently, a major donor had decided to shift their funding to other causes, which had left Bria and Hazel scrambling to find new sources of support.

"No—nothing new has happened in that department. And don't worry, I know that if we keep working on the problem, we'll find a solution. I wanted to talk to you about Caleb's replacement at St. Raymond's."

"Why would you need to talk to me about that?"

"Because they've found someone who can take over for him. Not permanently, but for a few weeks, so that they have time to conduct a thorough search for the new chief of obstetrics." Hazel sighed. "I've been dreading telling you this all morning, ever since I heard who it was. It's Eliot. Eliot Wright."

Bria almost dropped her coffee cup. "Eliot's coming back?" Her voice was barely a whisper.

"He's the one you used to date, isn't he?"

They'd been engaged, actually. Six years ago, she'd had a fiancé for less than a week—until her father had ruined everything.

Hazel looked mortified. "I didn't realize until this morning, or I swear I'd have told you sooner. Caleb never told me the new doctor's name. He just said it was an obstetrician from Boston, a good friend of his from when he did his residency there. And then this morning over breakfast I told him that you used to date a medical student who'd gone to Boston to finish his residency, and that's when Caleb told me a bit about the new doctor, and I realized it was *the* Eliot Wright. I was furious with Caleb for not telling me sooner, but he said—" Hazel abruptly cut herself off, as though she'd suddenly said too much.

"He said what?"

"He...said that Eliot had never mentioned you to him at all."

Bria tried not to feel hurt. She told herself that she didn't have any *right* to feel hurt. She'd broken up with him, after all.

Still. Had Eliot really not mentioned her to his friend at all?

Had he even thought of her again once he'd left for Boston?

She tried to regain her composure, for Hazel's sake. There was no need for her friend to look so worried. Six years was a long time. She and Eliot were ancient history. True, she was surprised to learn that he was coming back to Portland. But it was only surprise, not devastation, or grief, or any of the other terrible feelings she'd had when Eliot left. It wasn't as though she still had feelings for him.

When they'd broken up, she'd fallen into a deep well of heartbreak, and she'd spent most of the last six years climbing out of that well. It hadn't been easy, but she'd done it. She'd done it by focusing on the future, and by refusing to allow herself to dwell on painful memories.

It had been incredibly hard. She'd had to accept that Eliot was gone, and to let go of her dreams of the life they'd planned together. But, painful as it all had been, she'd managed to do it. And if he was back in Portland now, then she could not, would not allow his return to disrupt the hard-won stability she'd finally found here.

She'd had no reason to feel the pang that shot through her heart when Hazel said that Eliot had never mentioned her to Caleb. *I was just surprised to hear his name*, she thought.

"I'm really sorry," Hazel continued. "I should have asked Caleb more about his friend from Boston sooner. I should have realized that it might be Eliot."

"It's not your fault. Eliot and I dated before you and I met in nursing school. And there are a lot of obstetricians in Boston. There was no reason for you to guess it might be him." She probably shouldn't be surprised that Eliot hadn't talked to Caleb about her, either. Why would he ever bring up an ex-girlfriend to a close friend?

You told Hazel about him. True, but she had none of the difficulty with vulnerability that Eliot had. As she recalled, Eliot had rarely spoken of anything personal to anyone. He was a compassionate man with a deep desire for closeness, but he'd also built heavily fortified emotional walls for himself. His protective outer shell had been the source of so many of their problems. She'd longed to reach the inner warmth that she knew was there within him, but so often, his guardedness made that impossible. She was always left guessing at what he was thinking and feeling because he couldn't lower his defenses enough to let her know.

If he could, then maybe their breakup wouldn't have ended in the worst way possible.

They'd met shortly after she'd graduated college, when he was in his final year of medical school. They hadn't met on campus, but in her home: Eliot's mother cleaned houses for many of the families in Portland and had worked for Bria's father for years. Bria had often heard Eliot's mother speak of her son, who was going to be a doctor, but they'd never actually met until Eliot had appeared on her doorstep to give his mother a ride home. As Bria got to know him, she realized there was an authenticity to him that she hadn't felt with anyone else in her father's world, where everyone seemed preoccupied with their own wealth and self-importance.

They began dating, and things quickly became serious. They might have been young, but they both knew what they wanted. When Eliot asked her to come with him to Boston for his residency—as his wife—her response had been a heartfelt *yes*.

But then her father had interfered, as she should have known he would. The only thing Calvin Thomas loved more than money was control.

In addition to being the head of Portland's wealthiest family, Bria's father was also a retired surgeon. His wealth and privilege had given him lofty ideas of the respect due to the Thomas family. Both of Bria's sisters had lived up to their father's expectations and married men who came from families with generations of inherited wealth.

But Eliot's situation was different. He was raised by a single mother with very little money. He'd funded most of his education through scholarships and student loans. Calvin was convinced that Eliot's only interest in Bria was her family's fortune. Even if Eliot hadn't been deep in debt with student loans, there was the insurmountable fact of his background: Eliot simply wasn't good enough for her.

Bria didn't believe that for a minute. And when her father realized his threats to cut her off from the family trust wouldn't work, he changed tactics and threatened Eliot instead. He'd warned her that if she didn't break off her engagement, he'd do everything he could to ruin Eliot's career.

Bria knew her father would follow through with his threat. He was a major donor to numerous medical charities and sat on the board of more than one medical philanthropic organization. As a former surgeon, he still had connections in the medical field. If he'd made a concerted effort to hold Eliot back, she knew he would have been successful.

And she could not be an obstacle in Eliot's career. She knew how hard he'd worked, and how much his mother had sacrificed, to get him through medical school. She could not live with herself if she stood in the way of his success.

She couldn't tell him what her father had done, because Eliot wasn't the kind of man who backed down in the face of threats. But Eliot didn't know Calvin Thomas like she did. He didn't know what he was up against. Devastated as she was, she knew the safest course of action for him was for her to break things off with him and hope that he would find happiness with someone else.

She'd written him a note, an awful, horrible note, telling him that she'd changed her mind. They were from two different worlds, and they couldn't possibly be happy together. She'd tried to be convincing, because otherwise he'd find out she was lying to him, and then her father's threats would come out. But perhaps she'd not been convincing enough, because he'd shown up at her home, demanding to hear from her in person that she meant all that she'd written.

The result was an argument that grew far more heated than she'd expected. He accused her of being utterly selfish. He said he couldn't believe how shallow and materialistic she was. And even though she knew that, to an extent, his reaction was understandable, his accusations still hurt. She'd spent her life trying to prove that her privilege hadn't made her selfish, or materialistic, or proud, and now here was Eliot, a man she'd loved and trusted more than anyone, accusing her of being exactly those things. She tried not to fire back at him, because he didn't know the whole story, but his words had burned. And eventually she did lash out, because he knew where she was sensitive, and just what to say to shock her.

He'd told her that she was a naive, spoiled,

out-of-touch princess whose money insulated her from any real-life issues. She'd responded that she'd never realized what he really thought of her, or how cold and uncaring he could be. They'd traded insults for a while, and when they finally parted, it was with far more hurt and anger and pain on both sides than Bria would have ever thought possible.

She'd never known just how sensitive he was about her family's money and status, because he hadn't told her how he felt. Nor had she realized that he could see her exactly the way she'd always feared people would: as shallow and privileged, with no understanding of how the real world worked. Their marriage never would have worked with all that resentment locked inside him.

There was one silver lining to the breakup, despite all the misery involved. Breaking the engagement had given her a stark clarity about the amount of control her father and his money had over her life. She was determined that Calvin Thomas would never be able to control her or anyone else she cared about in that way again. And so she'd removed herself from her family's trust, despite her father's derisive assurances that she would never be able to survive on her own. She'd gotten a job and used the income from that and her personal savings to

pay for a nurse-midwifery program, where she'd
met Hazel. She'd managed to build a new life
for herself that was very different from the one
she'd had before, but she absolutely loved it. It
might be a smaller life, but it was all hers, and
she was proud of her independence.

She wasn't the same woman she'd been when
Eliot had last seen her. She was far more self-
possessed, far less naive and far more knowl-
edgeable of the world. So there was no reason
Eliot's return should disrupt her life. She'd managed to recover from all the hurt they'd caused
each other, and she hoped he had, too.

In fact, maybe it was a good thing that Eliot
was returning. How else would she be able to
prove to herself that she'd made peace with their
breakup unless they saw one another again?
Now that he was back, she'd have a chance to
greet him calmly, one medical professional to
another, and to show him all the confidence and
independence she'd gained. After six years, she
should be able to manage that.

"It's going to be fine," she told Hazel with all
the certainty she could muster. "Eliot and I have
been over for a long time, and I've never wished
him anything but a happy life of his own."

Hazel still looked skeptical.

"Really, Hazel. It'll be all right. Given the
amount of work we have at the center, I'm going

to be far too busy while he's here to dwell on the past."

As if to prove Bria's point, the emergency on-call phone began to buzz. "See?" Bria said, holding up the phone. "I barely have time to spend with *you*."

Hazel still looked unconvinced. "If you need a little time to process all this, Bria, I could take that call for you."

"Absolutely not," said Bria. "Duty calls, and anyway, it's your turn for a day off." She opened the phone. "Multnomah Falls Midwives," she said with a firm glance at Hazel that brooked no further negotiation. "How can I help?"

Even though it meant the end of her relaxing Saturday morning, Bria was grateful for the emergency call. Work had always been a refuge for her.

After the breakup with Eliot, she'd realized how desperate she was to escape her father's control. But she'd also realized how much she wanted to do something meaningful with her life. Calvin had been scornful of her decision to become a midwife. In his mind, midwifery wasn't as prestigious as becoming a surgeon. But Bria hadn't wanted prestige. Her mother had passed away when she was in college, and she'd found herself feeling drawn to the bond between mothers and newborns. There was something about the experience of birth that made her feel close to all mothers in general, and to her own mother in particular.

She couldn't imagine any career as rewarding as midwifery. Birth was a sacred ritual, shared by every human being. It was all the more meaningful if she could help women give birth in their homes, with their loved ones close at hand.

But babies had a way of coming in their own time, rather than when they were expected. And the Schroeder family's fifth baby was about to make its way into the world nearly a month early.

Bria raced to the Schroeder house, trying to keep her car within the speed limit. She'd asked Hazel to call for an ambulance to St. Raymond's before she left. She didn't anticipate any difficulties, as Mrs. Schroeder's pregnancy had progressed without complication—until now. Still, with a premature baby, it was best not to take any chances.

Mrs. Schroeder was inclined to agree. "It's too early," she said, her face worried as she clasped Bria's hand.

"Don't be afraid," Bria replied. "I've delivered babies earlier than this. We're going to be fine. But for now, I need you to start breathing, just as we practiced." She pulled back the sheets to begin her assessment and asked Mr. Schroeder to bring more towels.

As Bria felt for the baby's head, she felt a thick loop fall into her hand. Her blood ran cold. A prolapsed umbilical cord. She took in a long, slow breath, trying to steady herself. Thank goodness Hazel had already called the ambulance. Even now, she was relieved to hear sirens in the distance.

"What is it?" asked Mrs. Schroeder, noting Bria's worried expression. "What's wrong?"

Adrenaline rushed through Bria's veins, as it always did during a medical emergency. "The umbilical cord has dropped past the cervix and is coming out before the baby's head."

"Is that bad?" said Mr. Schroeder, who had returned.

"It's something we need to take care of right away," said Bria. A prolapsed cord was a serious emergency. Mrs. Schroeder needed to be transported to the hospital for a cesarean section as soon as possible.

Bria adopted her calmest demeanor. "Hear those sirens outside? Since Mrs. Schroeder went into labor so early, my colleague Hazel called an ambulance before I left. And that's a very good thing, as now we do need to get Mrs. Schroeder to the hospital right away. If you'll be so kind as

to head downstairs to let them in, Mr. Schroeder, then I can help Mrs. Schroeder until the
paramedics arrive." Mr. Schroeder nodded and
rushed downstairs.

"Now," said Bria to her patient, "it's very important that you don't push. We need to keep the
baby's head from pressing against the umbilical
cord. I'm going to hold the baby away from the
cord until we can get you to the hospital, where
they'll do a cesarean."

Mrs. Schroeder looked at her with pleading
eyes. "But you'll stay with me until then?"

Bria smiled. "All the way."

The ambulance would have Mrs. Schroeder
at the hospital within minutes, but until then,
her only option was to manually push the baby's head away from the umbilical cord until
they arrived.

She explained this to Mrs. Schroeder, who
grimaced. "I hope you've got strong arms."

"I do," Bria replied, with a wink. "But we'll
both have to be strong now. Your job is to keep
doing your breathing, stay relaxed and *not push*.
Meanwhile, I'm just going to hold the baby in
position for…for as long as it takes."

Bria kept her right arm extended, as still and
straight as she could make it. She wasn't sure
how long she could hold her arm like that. The
answer, she supposed, was for as long as was

necessary. No matter how tired her arm was, she wasn't going to let go of the baby's head.

Though how the paramedics were going to get her and Mrs. Schroeder down the stairs was a mystery.

One thing at a time, Bria told herself. *Focus on holding the baby's head for now. You can worry about the stairs later.*

She hadn't been lying when she'd told Mrs. Schroeder she had strong arms. She was a midwife; upper-arm strength came with the territory. But as a bead of sweat formed on her forehead, she couldn't help thinking that the sooner the paramedics reached them, the better.

She could feel the baby's pulse through the umbilical cord. The steady throb reassured her that the baby wasn't in distress. If she could keep holding the baby in position until the cesarean was performed, all would be well. Probably.

A clatter on the stairs informed her that help had arrived. "Prolapsed cord," Bria called as they entered the room. "I'm holding the head away from the cord."

"Great," said the first paramedic in the room. "Keep doing that." She addressed Mrs. Schroeder. "Ma'am, we need to get you down these stairs and out the door. So my colleagues and I are going to lift you onto this stretcher while your midwife keeps making sure the baby is getting enough oxygen."

"What does that mean?" asked Mrs. Schroeder.

"It means the three of you—mother, baby and midwife—are all about to go for a ride," the paramedic replied.

Climbing onto the stretcher between the knees of a pregnant woman, while holding a baby in position and keeping her right arm perfectly still, was a gymnastic feat Bria hadn't known she was capable of. The paramedics helped her find her footing as she focused on holding the baby's head in place.

"Don't be afraid, Mrs. Schroeder," Bria said as the paramedics lifted the stretcher and then tilted it to begin their descent down the stairs. "The good thing about going down these stairs is that it puts you exactly in the position we want. We need to keep your head below your feet to keep the pressure off the cord, right up until we can get baby out." That part was true enough: with a prolapsed cord, Mrs. Schroeder would need to give birth in Trendelenburg position, with her head tilted below her feet. It was just that the Trendelenburg position didn't typically involve mother and midwife both being hoisted into the air, the midwife unable to move one arm and clinging to the stretcher with the other for dear life.

Her right arm was aching now, but she didn't dare move it. By the time they arrived at the landing, both she and Mrs. Schroeder were covered in sweat.

"The hard part's over now," she said to Mrs. Schroeder. "Compared to getting down those stairs, driving to the hospital and getting baby out safely will be a breeze." Her arm was starting to go numb, but Bria barely felt it, bolstered by the adrenaline and the knowledge that they would be at St. Raymond's within minutes. She could hold this baby's head for five more minutes. She could hold it forever, if that was what it took to see it delivered safely.

Fortunately, forever wasn't necessary. The ambulance reached St. Raymond's in record time. The paramedics placed the stretcher holding Bria and Mrs. Schroeder onto a gurney, and they burst through the doors of the obstetrics department before Bria even had time to take note of her surroundings. She began shouting out the medical history to the obstetrician on duty the moment they entered the room.

"Multigravida in preterm labor, cervix dilated to—" And her voice faltered.

Because the obstetrician on duty was Eliot.

Eliot was already working at St. Raymond's.

As focused as she'd been on her patient while on the way to hospital, she hadn't had a moment to consider that she might be about to run into Eliot for the first time in six years. But now he stood in front of her. Just over six feet of tall, dark and handsome. His hair, so dark it was almost black, fell over his forehead, a few wayward strands brushing against familiar brown eyes. His body had always been lithe and graceful, but from the way his white coat outlined his shoulders, he seemed to have put on more muscle than when she'd last known him. His jaw was a firm, contoured line, but his lips were as alluring as she remembered.

Her traitorous heart was performing backflips. She'd tried so hard to convince both herself and Hazel that she was Completely Fine with Eliot working at St. Raymond's, but now it was obvious that she Completely Wasn't. Now that he was here, inches away from her, his body towering over her and smelling faintly of cinnamon, just as it always had, and his eyes were glowering at her with an intensity she couldn't recall ever seeing in them before.

"Well?" he barked. His voice brought her back into the room. "How long has she been having contractions? What's the fetal heart rate?"

Bria tried to respond, but it was as though the words couldn't get past her throat. She knew what she wanted to say—and her lips actually formed the words—but somehow, she couldn't get them out.

"Let's go," he said, a note of impatience entering his voice. She couldn't exactly blame him. She wanted to speak—she'd hadn't thought, that morning, that she would have any trouble speaking to him—but now, with all six feet two of him in the flesh beside her, she couldn't seem to find her voice.

He turned away, clearly exasperated. "We'll begin anesthesia immediately." Numerous nurses bustled about the room, preparing for surgery, drawing blood and setting up monitors for mother and baby.

Her right arm was very tired. She tried to distract herself from the numbing sensation spreading from her fingers to her elbow by thinking about other things. Clouds. Happy dogs. Coffee with Hazel. Exes that suddenly reappeared without warning.

She would not have moved her hand from the baby's head under any circumstances, but she would be damned if she failed in her duty as a midwife in front of Eliot Wright. Whatever else he thought of her, she was determined to make him see that she was competent and professional. She gritted her teeth and held her arm stiff and motionless.

She was so focused on keeping still that she didn't notice that Eliot had returned to her side.

"The baby's heart tones on the monitor look reassuring," he said. Bria let out a careful breath of relief at the news.

"Then there's no fetal distress?" She was pleased that she'd recovered her voice. As long as they kept their focus on the patient, she should be fine.

"So far, so good. You've done well. You'll only need to hold the head for a few minutes more."

Bria kept her arm straight as Eliot began the cesarean. *Just a little more*, she told herself. *You can make it through this. Just a little bit longer.*

Whether she was referring to her rapidly numbing arm, or standing near Eliot, she wasn't quite sure.

When he finally pulled the baby from Mrs. Schroeder's womb—a girl, with a healthy set of lungs—Bria felt the surge of tears that pricked at the corners of her eyes with every birth. She eased her arm back, rubbing her elbow to bring back circulation. For just a moment, she was lost in joy and relief as the other nurses patted her on the back and Eliot's familiar smile turned from the baby toward her.

But then their eyes met, and her heart sank as the smile faded from his face.

"Well," he said, gruffly. "A fine job done by all."

"Eliot," she began, without even the faintest idea of what she could say next.

"Excuse me," he cut in. "I need to see to other patients." And without another word, he left the room, leaving Bria with a numb feeling that had nothing to do with the stiffness in her arm.

CHAPTER TWO

ELIOT HAD SPENT nearly six years trying not to think about Bria Thomas. It hadn't been easy to recover from having his heart shattered into a million pieces, but he thought he'd done an admirable job of moving on with his life after Bria broke off their engagement. Once, he'd thought he wouldn't be able to live without her, but that was before he'd learned that she wasn't the person he'd thought she was.

Their lives were very different—she'd been the child of wealth and privilege, while he'd grown up among the wealthy, but not one of them. His first impression of Bria was that she was just another one of the snobbish elite who felt themselves better than Portland's working class, but as he'd gotten to know her better, he'd formed a different impression. She'd seemed down-to-earth, caring and adventurous, and he'd thought she was the woman he wanted to spend the rest of his life with.

They'd had one blissful year together before the night he learned just how wrong he'd been about her. Not only did she not want to marry him—she'd changed her mind only days after accepting his proposal—but during their breakup, she also confirmed his worst fear: that after growing up in such a rich and powerful family, a life with him wouldn't satisfy her. *Two different worlds*, she'd said. The phrase still infuriated him. There was only one world, and he'd thought they could find a place for both of them in it. But she'd made it clear that that wasn't what she wanted, and if she didn't want to marry him, there wasn't much he could do besides let her go.

Over the past six years, he'd finished his residency in Boston, started a private practice, participated in a few extremely successful business ventures and spent plenty of time *not* thinking about Bria. But not thinking about her was a lot easier when he wasn't working with her.

More than thirty-six hours had passed since his encounter with Bria, and he still felt shaken. He'd had no idea that she'd become a midwife, let alone that she was working at a women's health center across the street from St. Raymond's. He'd known there was a chance she might still live in Portland, but as he'd planned to spend most of his time at the hospital, he'd

JULIE DANVERS 35

thought avoiding her would simply be a matter of staying away from restaurants they used to go to. He'd assumed his chances of running into her were slim.

Apparently, his assumptions couldn't have been more wrong.

Any hope he had of avoiding her evaporated as he learned more about the close relationship between St. Raymond's and the Multnomah Falls Women's Health Center. The two facilities shared patients regularly. Not only was he not going to be able to avoid Bria, he'd probably have to work with her frequently.

And he had no idea yet how he was going to handle it.

He sat over his lunch in his office at St. Raymond's, glaring at his computer screen. Monday at noon, his schedule read. Tour of Multnomah Falls Women's Health Center.

Dr. Victor Anderson, the hospital's chief of staff, had urged him to get to know the center so that he would be familiar with the experiences of their shared patients when they arrived at St. Raymond's, and so he would know the layout of the center if he was called there for an emergency. It was a completely practical suggestion, yet Eliot couldn't help feeling as though the universe was conspiring to throw him into Bria's path. He was dreading the tour.

Come on, she's just an ex, he thought. *It's hardly the most stressful thing you'll face this week.*

He wished he could believe that was true. Over the weekend he'd dealt with two sets of twins and a placental abruption, but none of it had left him reeling as much as his encounter with Bria. He felt embarrassed by the brusque way he'd treated her on Saturday. No matter what was in their past, they were both medical professionals, and he should have acted accordingly. Eliot had great respect for midwives, who could afford to spend more time with their patients and often got to know them better than physicians. But by barking questions at Bria like he had, he'd probably come off as exactly the kind of elitist obstetrician he couldn't stand.

His curtness had been a clumsy attempt to cover his shock at seeing her again. Most people would have grown flustered by his manner. But instead of jumping to respond, Bria had remained silent, patiently waiting for him to settle down and address her more professionally. He'd been impressed, and a little ashamed, of the way she'd waited for him to collect himself. Fortunately, he'd been able to focus on the patient and the emergency at hand, but he was certain she'd noticed that it had taken a moment for him to recover from seeing her.

He couldn't believe how different she'd looked—and how familiar. Her dark brown hair was now cropped into a pixie cut, with short strands that framed her face and accentuated her large green eyes. He couldn't help noticing how well it suited her, even though a small part of him might secretly miss the feeling of running his hands through the tresses that once fell to her shoulders. Despite the surface changes, there was a warmth about her that felt the same as it ever had. She radiated a calmness about her that was almost palpable, even as an emergency swirled about them.

There had been a time when he'd taken great comfort in that calmness. Trusted it enough to open up to her in a way he'd never opened himself to anyone before. He wouldn't make the same mistake again.

For years, Eliot had tried to avoid ruminating over their breakup, but now the memories came racing back. She could have given him any number of reasons for breaking off their engagement, but she'd chosen the one that would hurt worst of all. She'd told him that she'd realized they couldn't relate to one another because they were from different worlds. She'd meant that she was accustomed to the finer things in life, things that he would probably never grow to appreciate, no matter how hard he worked or how successful he became. And the fact of their different backgrounds was something that would never change, no matter what other work they put into their relationship.

At first, he couldn't believe those words were coming from her. He was certain her father had influenced her. He knew Calvin Thomas—his mother had introduced him to the man in high school, thinking that her son who wanted to be a doctor might benefit from getting to know a renowned retired surgeon. And Calvin, flattered, had paternalistically taken Eliot aside and given him advice about how to prepare for medical school. Even then, Calvin had struck Eliot as a pompous man with an inflated sense of self-importance. And years later, when he'd begun dating Bria, he found that Calvin still held rigid, outdated ideas about class differences.

But Bria had often criticized her father for holding those opinions, for caring so much about money, and so it had come as a complete surprise to suddenly hear her parroting his words. She'd insisted that they were her own words—that her father hadn't pressured her or threatened her. She'd thought it over, she'd said, and there were just too many reasons their relationship wouldn't work. He couldn't afford to give her the kind of lifestyle she was used to. True, she could buy things on her own, but would a man as proud as Eliot really be comfortable with an arrangement like that? The condescension in her voice had galled him. And her words had hurt all the more because they rang true: he didn't want Bria to pay for everything in their lives. He didn't want to be her prince consort, hovering in the background while she made all the financial decisions.

The more he'd felt as though she was talking down to him, the more heated their conversation became, until eventually they were shouting at each other. Finally, he'd pleaded with her that even though he might not be able to afford the lifestyle she was used to, at least they'd have each other.

Yes, she'd responded, *but we wouldn't have anything else.*

It had been those words, more than anything, that finally convinced him that she meant it when she said she didn't love him and had changed her mind about marrying him. He'd thought, perhaps hoped, that her father was behind her decision, but he didn't think she would try to cut him so deeply unless the way she felt about him really had changed.

And so he'd left. Moved on. Tried to accept that he was probably better off without someone who'd turned out to be so materialistic and shallow. He wouldn't make the same mistake of trusting her again. Even if he did have to work with her for the next few weeks.

At least she seemed to be a competent midwife. No matter what bitterness he might feel about their breakup, he had to admit he was impressed with how she'd responded to her patient's crisis. The way she'd held that baby perfectly in place—God only knew how long she'd been holding the head before reaching the hospital. Her arm must have been terribly sore. But she'd done what was required, without complaint. And she'd seemed genuinely concerned for her patient. He recalled the relief in her eyes when he'd reassured her there was no sign of fetal distress. She'd always had such large, expressive eyes. And now that he had a moment to think about it, other memories came to mind: memories of those eyes staring at him over a pillow, of her arms reaching for him…

He couldn't let himself indulge in old memories. His time at St. Raymond's was supposed to give him six weeks immersed in the medical world so that he could make a decision about his future. He couldn't do that if he got distracted by Bria's eyes, however alluring they might be.

When Caleb had called to ask if he'd be interested in taking over the obstetrics department at St. Raymond's for a few weeks, he'd jumped at the chance. It had been a few years since he'd done any hospital work, and he missed it. His career hadn't turned out the way he'd expected. His original plan had been to go to medical school and discover his calling, which turned out to be obstetrics. Unfortunately, he'd quickly learned that while medicine might be a path to a fulfilling career, it was no guarantee of wealth, and Eliot had needed money.

Between his medical school loans and his desire to provide for the single mother who'd raised him, he couldn't wait the ten or fifteen years it took for most doctors to begin earning a large income. And so he'd turned to business, using his knowledge of the medical field to guide his investments.

Those investments had paid off more than he could have hoped, and now managing them was almost a full-time job. He still spent a few hours a week at his private practice, assisting with difficult cases or supervising new trainees. His business partners had urged him to give up his medical license entirely, arguing that delivering babies was costing him money. His tax attorney said that if he quit medicine and spent that time working on his portfolio instead, he'd easily make another million, maybe two million each year. But Eliot couldn't bring himself to quit obstetrics completely. He loved being a doctor.

It was nice to have the security that money brought him, especially as it was something he'd never known growing up. But being a doctor brought him a sense of fulfilment that the business world had never been able to provide. No matter how much money he made, there was nothing as powerful as helping a new life come into the world. Obstetrics made him feel connected to a part of life that seemed truly magical, and giving it up would be like abandoning part of his identity. Working at St. Raymond's felt like a vacation compared to his days spent reading market reports and analyzing profits.

The senior partners at his firm hadn't been pleased when he'd announced he would be taking six weeks off to work at a hospital. They'd only agreed to it because he'd gotten another doctor to cover his private practice patients while he was away, and he knew they were hoping that he would leave his practice for good once he returned to Boston. One partner had even told him they were looking forward to Eliot "getting medicine out of his system once and for all."

As much as Eliot loved medicine, it *was* becoming increasingly difficult to balance both of his careers. He was at a crossroads, and he didn't know what to do. Caleb's call had come at the perfect time. Six weeks working full-time at a hospital would help him feel more certain about what he wanted to do with the rest of his career.

He'd intended to spend his time at St. Raymond's finding answers to his questions about the future. Instead, he'd been put face-to-face with his past.

And now, instead of focusing on his career and what he wanted to do about it, he was stressing over how he was going to deal with seeing Bria again.

It's only for six weeks. You can do anything for six weeks.

As uncomfortable as it had been, Saturday's emergency had proven that he and Bria could put personal feelings aside and focus on patient care. If they'd done it once, they could continue doing it until he left Portland for good. He'd never had plans to stay, and he was eager to leave the moment his obligation to his friend was complete. If he wanted to ensure a smooth exit, then the best thing he could do would be to make it clear that he was a professional who didn't let personal issues get in the way of his work.

In fact, he decided that he was *glad* Dr. Anderson had scheduled his tour of the Women's Health Center for today. The sooner he ran into Bria again, the sooner he'd be able to demonstrate in no uncertain terms he felt no differently about working with her than he would with any other midwife.

He thought about Bria's green eyes again and swallowed. He wanted very much to prove to her that he wasn't at all affected by seeing her again. But a small part of him thought that he might need a chance to prove it to himself, too.

Bria was in a meeting with Hazel, their heads bent together over budget spreadsheets, when they were interrupted.

"There's a Dr. Wright at the reception desk." Joan, one of the students who staffed the front desk, stuck her head into the doorway. "He's been scheduled for a tour."

Bria groaned inwardly. The day was already off to a rough start, as she and Hazel had spent the morning taking a closer look at the center's financial situation, and they were becoming increasingly concerned at what they found. Eliot's arrival would have been difficult for Bria under the best of circumstances, but at the moment, it was a particularly unwelcome surprise.

"Did you know anything about this?" she asked Hazel.

"Not at all. I'd have given you some warning, I swear."

"Dr. Anderson called and asked if their new

interim chief of obstetrics could take a tour of the center, so I scheduled one for today. I'm so sorry if it's not a good time."

"Not at all, Joan." Bria mentally kicked herself. She should have seen this coming. All of the hospital's obstetrics staff had toured the center at one time or another, just as she'd needed to become familiar with the layout of the hospital when she'd first started. No one wanted to have to waste time searching for the right office or operating room when they were dealing with a pregnant patient in crisis.

"Joan, let Dr. Wright know we'll be out in just a moment," said Hazel. When Joan had shut the office door behind her, she said, "Bria, if you need me to, I can give Eliot the tour."

Bria felt her spine stiffen. As much as she dreaded facing Eliot after Saturday's fiasco, letting Hazel give the tour felt far too much like hiding. She was going to have to see Eliot again at some point, and she didn't want to wait until the next crisis arose. Better to establish their working relationship on her own turf, without a pressing emergency.

"That won't be necessary," she said. "You've got more than enough work for today."

"Still, I'm right here if you need anything," Hazel said. "And you and I are meeting up for a postmortem after work tonight, is that understood? Even if one of us has to work late and it's a virtual meet-up."

"I'll be fine," Bria insisted. She poked her head outside to look down the hallway. There he was, chatting with another receptionist. Though the hallway was long, she could faintly pick up on the deep tones of his voice. She could remember exactly how it felt to be wrapped in those long arms of his, her head pressed against his body, his baritone voice resonating through his chest.

That's not helpful, she thought, willing herself to ignore the memories. Since Saturday, she'd had some time to think about how she would cope with Eliot's presence over the next few weeks. When they'd parted, he'd accused her of being materialistic and self-centered. And despite his understandable reasons for making those accusations, the words had hurt her deeply. Eliot might think that that her privilege blinded her to the realities of life, and maybe—though she hated to admit it—maybe there had been a time in her life when that was true. But that wasn't who she was anymore. She'd worked hard to build her career as a midwife, and if she wanted Eliot to respect her as a professional, then she'd need to act professional. Which meant not allowing herself to be distracted by that resonant voice of his. Or by the memories of being pulled close within those strong arms.

She forced herself to put on a warm, professional smile and headed toward the reception desk.

As she approached, she saw that he was holding a familiar blue box. Despite her nerves, her smile became more genuine.

"You brought donuts from Donut Stop Believing!" She cracked the box open, and the familiar scent of vanilla icing wafted out. "There's even—oh my god, is that a passion fruit cake donut?" The upscale bakery a few blocks away was a familiar treat from her past life; the bakery made some of the most outrageous—and expensive—donuts in the city. Now that her financial situation had changed, donuts this pricey no longer made it into her regular rotation of creature comforts.

She tried not to read too much into the fact that he'd remembered one of her favorite treats. It was probably mere coincidence, as doctors from St. Raymond's brought baked goods and lunches for the center's staff all the time. It was all part of networking.

"They're for your staff," he said, his voice cool and businesslike. "I thought they might enjoy something special."

"They certainly work hard enough to deserve

it," she replied, taking the box from him and setting it behind the counter. As she did, her fingers brushed against his, their first physical contact in six years, and her heart gave an unexpected jolt. *Move it along*, she thought. The sooner she got the tour underway, the less time she'd have to spend noticing how his dark eyes stood out against his white medical coat.

As she grabbed a clipboard from the reception desk and ushered him into the hallway, she again caught a faint waft of cinnamon. She'd thought it was from the donut box, but now she knew it was him. He used to enjoy a dash of cinnamon in his coffee, and evidently, he still did. The scent teased at her nose.

Yep, definitely need to get this over and done with.

"I'll give you the five-cent tour," she said, trying to keep her voice steady.

"I've been curious to see this place," he said. "Everyone at St. Raymond's has been singing your praises. I understand that things got off to a somewhat rocky start, but now it seems that the hospital finds the center to be indispensable."

She appreciated his comment about the center, but his tone was unmistakably cool. It was one thing to be professional; it was another to keep his voice entirely devoid of emotion. Did he really expect her to believe that he wasn't having any reaction to the utterly surreal situation in which they now found themselves? If there was one person she never thought she'd be taking on a tour of her center, it was Eliot. He had to feel *something* about seeing her again.

But if he did, he clearly wasn't going to show it. That fit with what she remembered about him. Rule number one in the Eliot Wright playbook: hide your feelings at all costs.

Well. If he wanted to act as though this situation was completely normal, no different from a tour of any other health center, then that was his prerogative. She matched his cool, informational tone.

"We do share patients quite a bit. For uncomplicated pregnancies, women are able to give birth here at the center, or at home if they prefer, but it's best for more complicated cases to move to the hospital for delivery. Case in point—here's Mrs. Patterson." A heavily pregnant woman in a blue dress had just left one of the exam rooms. "Sandra Patterson, meet Dr. Eliot Wright. He's chief of obstetrics at St. Raymond's."

"Interim chief," Eliot corrected. "It's just for the next six weeks."

"Six weeks?" Sandra laughed. "Then it sounds like we'll be meeting again."

"Mrs. Patterson is expecting quintuplets,"

Bria explained. Despite her determination to match Eliot's coolness, excitement crept into her voice. Everyone at the center was looking forward to the delivery of the quints.

"Any day now," Sandra affirmed. She let out a long exhalation. "I've just had the loveliest massage. Nobody who talks about the miracle of life ever brings up just how much lower back pain is involved in miracles."

"I hope you're feeling better now," said Bria.

"Goodness, loads better," Sandra replied. "I don't know what I'd do if it weren't for this place."

"Should a woman expecting quintuplets really be getting services at a birthing center?" Eliot frowned as he watched Sandra go. "Surely a hospital is the best place for her."

"Mrs. Patterson is the perfect example of the kind of patients we share. You're absolutely right that she should give birth at the hospital. But until then, what's wrong with letting her take full advantage of more holistic, integrative approaches? If you were about to give birth to five children, wouldn't you feel better with some massage or aromatherapy from time to time?"

"If I were giving birth to five children, I don't think all the aromatherapy in the world would be enough to make me feel better."

She gave him a sidelong glance, and for a split second, she thought they both might be about to laugh. Or share a smile, at the very least. But the moment passed almost as soon as it had begun, as they both made a hasty retreat back into their professional shells.

"Yes. Well. You're probably not wrong," she said, trying to collect herself. Once, it had felt so easy to be in his presence. This stiff formality between them didn't feel right at all. And yet it didn't seem as though she had any alternative.

She walked him past the clinical offices, describing the care they offered to patients, and paused when they reached the larger rooms down the hall. "We try to offer everything our pregnant patients could hope for in a birthing center and beyond. Prenatally, we offer everything from acupuncture to yoga. Down *that* hallway are some of our therapy rooms. We have counselors on staff to treat postpartum depression. And, of course, we have a pool for water births."

She saw an apprehensive look cross his face, and she hastily added, "I know the medical research is mixed on water births. But lots of single case studies point out that buoyancy makes it easier for mothers to shift position during labor."

"It's not that," he said. "It's just that you offer

quite a range of holistic services. I'm very impressed, but…"

"But what?"

"Who pays for all this? Unless you serve incredibly upscale clientele, then I can't imagine how an operation like this could keep running for very long. And I know that many of the hospital's patients couldn't afford a facility like this."

"Actually, we're able to offer care to every patient who walks through our doors, regardless of their ability to pay."

"Ah. Of course. I forgot who I'm talking to."

"Excuse me?"

"It's just that I'm sure it helps to provide state-of-the-art services when you have a family fortune to finance everything."

Bria felt a burst of irritation. She supposed it was natural for him to assume that she'd founded the center with her father's money, but the assumption rankled deeply. She and Hazel had spent countless hours on fund-raising, researching grant proposals and conducting community outreach programs. The center was hers, she had been there for every step of its formation and she was not going to have its success attributed to her father.

"Actually, the center subsists solely off grants and private donations, as well as what our clients pay when they can afford it. It's completely self-sufficient, and my father's money has nothing to do with it. I haven't even spoken to him in years."

She felt a pang of guilt as she realized that what she'd said about the center's self-sufficiency wasn't entirely truthful at the moment, considering her conversation with Hazel just a moment ago about their recent shortfall of funds, but she decided that was a detail she didn't need to mention immediately.

"Really?" The expression of surprise on his face was gratifying, but also irritating. He didn't need to look *so* shocked.

"Yes, really," she said, her voice coming out more sharply than she meant it to. "I may have had some things in life handed to me, but not this." She cringed inwardly over her choice of words. He'd said almost those exact words to her during their final, terrible argument: that she couldn't understand him because she'd had everything handed to her instead of working for it.

But if he noticed, he didn't mention it. He held up his hands. "I'm sorry. I'm sure it took a lot of work to make all of this possible." She suddenly felt foolish. Based on what Eliot knew about her, it was completely natural for him to assume she'd built the center with her father's help. He hadn't been trying to bring up the past, and she should steer clear of it as well.

"The center's very important to me," she said, hoping she could think of a way to explain her strong reaction that wouldn't bring up the past. "I didn't mean… You don't have to…" She hesitated, unable to find her words while Eliot maintained his cool, unemotional gaze. Dammit, if he'd just give her a clue about what he was feeling, this wouldn't be so hard. Finally, it was too much. "For God's sake, Eliot, are we really going to pretend as though this is a normal situation? Are we going to act like we don't have anything else to talk about?"

"What else should we be talking about?"

She fought the impulse to smack him with her clipboard. "How about the fact that we're here, working together, when we both thought we'd probably never see each other again?"

A look of pain flashed across his eyes, and for the first time that day, she saw his professional shell begin to crack. "That's right," he said. "Neither of us thought we'd see each other again. But now that we have, I don't see what difference it makes. We may have a past, but I think the best thing for both of us will be to let it stay there." Whatever she might have seen in his eyes a moment ago was gone. He'd reverted back to his detached, unemotional self.

"Then your plan is to just ignore it? Act like our engagement never happened?"

"My plan is to be professional," he replied. "I don't live in the shadow of my mistakes. I came here for six weeks to help out a friend, and that's still what I plan to do. There's no reason you and I shouldn't be able to work well together as colleagues for a while. So, no, I don't plan to 'pretend' this is a normal situation. I'm going to *treat* it like a normal situation, because that's what it is. You and I are no different from any other doctor and midwife working together."

His brisk, businesslike tone made her reel, but only for a moment. It hurt to think that he could so easily dismiss what had once been between them. But as much as she disliked his tone, she agreed with his words. For once, Eliot's tendency to put up emotional walls might be the right step forward for both of them. If they were going to work together, it would probably be better not to delve into the past. They needed to focus on their patients, not their personal issues.

But six weeks of seeing Eliot? Six weeks of pretending that it was completely normal to work with someone with whom she shared such an intimate history? Not to mention that he was every bit as attractive as she remembered. Seeing him had stirred up memories she hadn't attended to in quite some time, memories of heated nights together and long, luxurious mornings…

"Perfect," she said, trying to sound as though she meant it. "That's what I want, too. For the two of us to work together just as we would with any of our other colleagues." That part was true. She *did* want to work well with Eliot. She did want him to respect her as a professional.

It was just that being in such close proximity to him reminded her of times when she'd wanted other things, too. Like his smile directed at her. His arms wrapped around her. The warmth of his body close to hers.

After seeing him twice in only a few days, she'd found herself having to work harder at putting thoughts like that out of her mind than she had in years.

It was going to be a long six weeks.

CHAPTER THREE

THE NEXT DAY, Eliot was back in his office, hitting refresh on his computer screen.

He was trying very hard to keep his internet search focused on medical journal articles, but it was difficult to focus when images of Bria kept popping into his mind.

Don't look her up, he thought.

People look up their exes online all the time, his mind countered.

Not after six years.

He'd never bothered trying to see what Bria was up to before. After their breakup, he'd avoided all signs of her. He'd wanted to move on as quickly as possible, and looking her up online seemed to run counter to that plan.

But their conversation yesterday continued to nag at the back of his mind. The way her eyes blazed when he'd mistakenly assumed her father had paid for the Women's Health Center.

She hadn't spoken to her father in years, she'd said. Why not? Was it because of their breakup?

Even if it was, that didn't change the past. It couldn't erase what they'd said to each other during those final, awful moments.

Although Bria herself seemed to have changed. He'd never seen her eyes look like that before.

The memories of their relationship had flooded his mind over the past few days. The way her head fit right under his chin when she stood close to him. The softness of her skin against his fingers. The taste of vanilla lip balm and the smell of coffee that wafted from her.

She was still one of the most attractive women he'd ever met. Even now, after all that had happened between them, he couldn't help feeling something in his chest quicken when he'd watched her approach the reception desk yesterday. But he'd learned his lesson six years ago. He hadn't been good enough for her then. He didn't know whether learning that he was now a millionaire several times over would change how she felt about him, and he didn't care to know. If his money made him more attractive to her, then she wasn't the kind of person he wanted to be to be with.

But that fire in her eyes. She'd had the look of someone who'd had to fight hard for something.

The Bria he knew had never had to fight for anything, because she'd already had everything.

He wondered what else about her had changed.

The internet beckoned.

If he wanted to know about her life, he should ask her, he thought. He shouldn't be a creepy internet stalker.

But didn't people *expect* to research one another online? And now that he'd run into Bria again, it was only natural to be curious about what had happened in her life.

Five minutes later, he was scrolling through a list of search results.

There was the usual handful of articles on Bria's family from the gossip pages. Members of the Thomas family were always getting into the news for one reason or another, whether it was because they'd made some huge charitable donation, or because of more licentious behavior. But there was a surprising absence of articles that specifically mentioned Bria. Almost any mention of her seemed to be in connection with the center. What else had she been doing for the past six years?

That was when he saw the image that made his heart stop.

There was a paparazzi-style photo of Bria in a wedding dress, outside Abernethy Chapel, surrounded by her family.

She was married?

He clicked through the pictures, willing himself to stop.

Oh. His heart, which had been jackhammering in his chest, slowed with relief. Upon closer inspection, the woman in the wedding dress was one of Bria's sisters. Bria had just been a bridesmaid.

Ridiculous, he thought, as his heart rate settled. He had no reason to get so worked up over what Bria might or might not have done over the past six years. Why should he care about whether she'd been with anyone else? He hadn't exactly been celibate.

He shut his computer screen. He'd made it clear yesterday that he would treat her like any other medical colleague. And he wouldn't be poking around in the history of any other colleague online. This foolishness had to stop, immediately.

But try as he might, he couldn't stop the questions from swirling in his mind. What was Calvin Thomas's privileged daughter doing working as a midwife? She was obviously proud of building her career. But was she aware of how he'd built his?

Eliot had had to fight for most things in his life. Growing up, he'd attended one of Portland's most elite prep schools on extensive financial aid, because his mother couldn't afford the high tuition fees on her own. She cleaned houses for most of the wealthy families in the area, families who sent their children to the school Eliot attended.

His father had only been in his life intermittently and left for good when he was twelve. Before he did, he gave Eliot one piece of advice. "Don't let them know you're a scholarship student," he'd said. "In fact, don't tell them anything about yourself unless you absolutely have to. These people already think they're better than you. Don't give them any proof." And so Eliot had kept his scholarship a secret, and he'd told no one that he lived on the edge of town in a run-down apartment complex. He quickly saw that it was a necessary survival strategy, because his father was right. The other students did bully each other based on how much money they had and whose family was the most well-known. Any personal information he revealed risked making him a target. He'd learned to blend in and to keep his real thoughts and feelings to himself.

But he could only delay the inevitable for so long. Eventually, the truth got out among his classmates: that he wasn't a boarding student, his parents didn't fail to attend school functions because they were traveling abroad and he wasn't looked after by servants while they were away. He lived in a one-bedroom apartment with his single mother, who was so poor that she could barely afford to buy him more than one school uniform.

They teased him relentlessly. Anything that made him seem the least bit different was interpreted as a sign of poverty. His hair, the bologna sandwiches his mother packed in his lunches, his plain shoes. He hadn't cared what they thought of him, but he did take it as a valuable lesson in trust. His father had been right: anything he revealed about himself, anything that people in power perceived as different, was an opportunity for them to put him down. Trusting anyone, or revealing anything about himself, was asking for disaster.

Even in college and medical school, his father's prediction turned out to be true. The bullying wasn't as overt as when he'd been a child, but even as an adult, he could see how people who were privileged protected their own. He'd made some good friends, people who were working their way through and scraping by on student loans. Most of them, like his friend Caleb, were down-to-earth people who'd chosen medicine as a career because they cared deeply about helping others. But he'd also met a surprising number of people who seemed as though they were only interested in medicine because their families were pushing them toward a career with prestige. Those were the students who didn't seem particularly excited about medicine, yet who often seemed to get coveted training positions and well-paying jobs immediately after medical school because of their parents' connections.

Bria had been a breath of fresh air—at first. She might have come from exactly the kind of family he resented, but she was nothing like them. He'd thought she was authentic, genuine and compassionate. That was why it had hurt so much to find out that she did care about where he came from, after all.

Calvin Thomas had overheard every word of their final, vehement argument. As Eliot had stormed out of the Thomas mansion, Calvin had waylaid him in the foyer, and beckoned Eliot into the office.

"How much?" Calvin had said, bringing out his checkbook.

"How much for what?" Eliot replied, confused.

"How much to keep you from smearing the family name? I'm well aware of your financial situation, boy. If you can't get what you need from my daughter by marriage, I'm sure you'll find another way, and I don't want you running to the tabloids or the gossip sites. I want to know your price to keep all this quiet."

Eliot was aghast. At first, he couldn't respond. All he could do was gape.

"Come on, out with it," Calvin continued. "Everybody has their price. After four years of medical school, I'm guessing yours is about two hundred and fifty thousand dollars."

It was almost the exact amount of his student loans. But he didn't want money from Calvin. He'd always planned to pay the loans back himself, no matter how long it took.

"I don't need your money," he said.

"But I need your silence, and I want to make sure that I get it. All I ask is that you sign this nondisclosure agreement—" he pulled a document from his desk drawer "—and the money's yours."

Eliot hesitated. He couldn't believe that Calvin had a nondisclosure agreement drawn up and ready to be signed. Calvin noted his hesitation. "It was only practical to have this ready," he said, nudging the form toward Eliot. "It could never have lasted between you two. I always told her that, and she's had the good sense to finally see it."

He wrote out a check and handed it to Eliot. "Don't be stupid, boy. Your loans will be coming due soon. It's not easy to make the payments on a young doctor's salary. All you have to do is keep your mouth shut, and the money's yours."

Eliot had taken great pleasure in ripping up that check and continuing on his way out the door. Calvin didn't need to worry about him badmouthing the Thomas family to the press. He never wanted to talk or think about any of them ever again.

He'd thought that was the end of the matter. But then his mother had gotten a Christmas bonus from the Thomas family. A check for two hundred and fifty thousand dollars.

His mother was overjoyed. When he saw how happy she was, he couldn't bring himself to tell her about the argument between him and Bria. He'd only told her that the engagement was off. She'd offered to stop working at the Thomas house, but Eliot couldn't let her do that; the Thomas family was one of her best customers. He couldn't let his mother deprive herself of that income when he knew how much she needed it.

She'd cleaned the Thomas mansion for fifteen years, and she'd assumed that Mr. Thomas was giving her this unexpected windfall to pay for Eliot's tuition. It even said in the memo, "For fifteen years of loyal service."

He'd never seen her so proud. "You see?" she'd said. "People notice when you work hard. I've always put in little extra touches for the families I work for, and even though they never said anything, I know they noticed." She was beaming; he could tell how much it meant to her to feel valued and appreciated.

He knew, too, how much his mother wanted to help him pay for medical school. He couldn't bear to tell her what the money really meant. Calvin's trap had been extremely effective: Eliot might not have signed the nondisclosure agreement, but he also couldn't tell the truth about the money without having to reveal to his mother that it had nothing to do with their appreciation for her hard work at all. She'd thought it was a genuine bonus, while he knew it was just hush money. After everything she'd sacrificed for him, he refused to take away one iota of her pride.

His mother had insisted on using the money to pay off his medical school loans, even though he'd protested that she should keep it for herself. She wouldn't hear a word of it, and Eliot graduated medical school debt-free, with a little extra money to spare. When his mother had refused even that small amount, Eliot had invested it instead. Those investments had been successful and formed the basis of Eliot's multimillion-dollar fortune today.

For years, he'd tried to tell himself that he owed Calvin Thomas nothing. But that wasn't the whole truth, no matter how hard he tried to convince himself otherwise. He felt guilty for judging Bria's wealthy background when, in the end, he'd benefited from her family's fortune just as much as she had.

He knew how Calvin Thomas's mind worked. He'd wanted Eliot to know that he'd never have been able to make his fortune without Calvin's help. Even if he'd paid the man back, it wouldn't change his situation now. If Calvin hadn't written that check, Eliot would still be struggling to pay off his medical school debts. He'd never have been able to make his investments at the time he did, nor would he have amassed his own wealth, without Calvin's help. He'd tried to alleviate his guilt by doing good with the money. As soon as he'd earned his first million, he'd funded his mother's immediate retirement, and he gave freely to many charities. But nothing could ever change the fact that he owed his entire fortune to Calvin Thomas, and it was a bitter pill to swallow. He suspected Calvin knew exactly how much Eliot hated that.

And something about those blazing eyes of Bria's told him that she would hate it, too.

Bria obviously took great pride in having built her business without her father's help. What would she think if she knew that he hadn't been able to do the same? Or was it possible that she already knew, and the blaze in her eyes had held some scorn for him? He didn't think so. Bria had seemed more defensive than anything. If she'd known about Calvin's "donation," she'd have mentioned it yesterday. And it shouldn't matter if she found out. It wasn't as though her judgment of him mattered in any way. It was simply a matter of personal pride. He preferred that she didn't know what he owed to Calvin. But that didn't make her stand out: he preferred that *no one* knew what he owed to Calvin. Which was in keeping with his determination to treat her like any of his other colleagues.

If Bria didn't know, then there was no reason for him to bring it up now. It was far in the past, and it wasn't as though he gave detailed reports to his other colleagues on how he'd made his fortune. He'd just tried not to think about it. The same way he tried not to think of the memories of certain intimate nights together. Or the way she still tilted her head in thought, exposing the delicate curve of her neck. Those things were private. What was one more secret in the face of things?

Bria stepped outside the delivery room at St. Raymond's and tore off her gloves, welcoming the coolness of the air against her hands. The labor she'd just assisted with had lasted for almost ten hours, and her lower back was aching. She tried to ease the knots out of her shoulders as she leaned against the wall. Sometimes, when she witnessed the miracle of life, she thought the real miracle would be if the baby could come out quickly.

She raised her head to glance into the window of the delivery room door—Mrs. Hatfield and her baby boy were gazing deeply into one another's eyes. Despite her exhaustion, Bria smiled. She would never be tired of seeing the expression on a parent's face when greeting a new life for the first time.

Familiar footsteps sounded behind her. Eliot joined her at the window, bending down to peer in. "It never gets old, does it?"

She gave a rueful smile. Lately, witnessing the first few bonding moments between parents and their children was bittersweet, as she'd begun to feel less certain of ever experiencing such a moment herself. Still, she knew she could never stop watching. The privilege of being present at those early moments was by far one of the best professional perks of being a midwife.

Not that she could voice any of this to Eliot. The two of them had worked well together over the past few days, but their focus had been entirely on patients. Eliot had stuck to his resolution to ignore their past and treat her like any other colleague. She, however, was well aware of Eliot's presence having an effect on her—she'd caught herself casting glances over the muscles that lined his chest and upper arms, which definitely hadn't been there six years ago. She tried not to notice, but she did, and couldn't help getting caught up in dwelling on how those muscular arms might feel when wrapped around her waist. She'd had every intention of treating him like any other doctor.

Though Eliot clearly wasn't *just* any other doctor—and not just because of their history. Even though he'd only been at St. Raymond's for a few days, she'd had the chance to see him in action more than once. He was supremely skilled, and his intuition alerted him to complications that might be overlooked by less sensitive physicians. He was a doctor she'd have been proud to work with under any other circumstances, and she found herself respecting him on a professional level.

And on an unprofessional level, if she did happen to notice those newly defined chest muscles…well, she'd just have to suffer in silence.

But Mrs. Hatfield's new baby should be a safe topic, falling firmly into the professional realm they'd agreed to share. She yawned and rubbed her back. "It never gets old, but midwives get tired. Poor Mrs. Hatfield started her contractions at ten this morning."

Eliot winced in sympathy. "You must be tired."

She stifled another yawn. "I was just about to head to the hospital commissary for a cup of coffee." She hesitated, wondering if she should invite him along. He'd brought her donuts on Monday. True, he'd made it clear that they were professional networking donuts, but maybe he'd receive her offer of coffee in the same vein. She wanted to extend an olive branch. She'd do anything to end this awful, stilted formality. They could be polite without being cold to each other, couldn't they?

"Would you like to join me?" She blurted the words out before she could overthink them.

He raised his eyebrows. "Are you sure that's a good idea?

"Look, you're the one who said we're no different from any other doctor and midwife working together. If you were any other doctor, I'd invite you to grab a coffee and ask how you were settling in."

He still hesitated, and at first she thought he was going to refuse. But then he said, "Fair enough. I suppose if you were any other midwife, I'd accept."

He was being so cautious, she thought with a wave of sadness. And yet, what else could she expect from him? She'd been the one to end their relationship. It made sense that he'd be hesitant to spend any time with her again.

The hospital commissary was abuzz with medical staff who were consulting on cases, sharing jokes and generally enjoying one another's company. Bria and Eliot got their drinks and sat down. She looked at his coffee cup and wrinkled her nose. "Is that…decaf?"

He laughed, and as he did, his face lit up for a moment with all the warmth and energy that had attracted her years ago. "The cost of getting a few years older. That, and I'm not used to these long hospital shifts. I've been relying on coffee a lot more since I started here at St. Raymond's, but I try to make every other cup decaf, so I don't go tachycardic."

"Wait, do you mean you don't work at a hospital out in Boston?"

"I haven't worked in a hospital since my residency."

She couldn't hide her surprise. He was so talented. When they'd dated, he'd been about to graduate medical school near the top of his class. Any hospital should have been thrilled to have him on staff.

"I went into private practice right away. It was the only way I could balance both my careers."

"You're not just an obstetrician?"

"I manage a firm that deals in medical holdings and investments. As you can imagine, it takes up quite a lot of time. I could never combine that with a medical career on a hospital's schedule."

She'd never pictured him in the business world. He'd always been so committed to medicine, so driven to succeed as a physician. But she was glad that he'd done well for himself.

"And you're…happy with that balance?"

He mulled this over. "Satisfied, I suppose? I've accepted it. Money is a necessary evil in American health care, and being invested in the business side of things gives me a different perspective on what my patients are facing. But it's getting more difficult to do both, so I'm thinking of giving up medicine."

She nearly dropped her coffee cup. Becoming a doctor had been a lifelong dream for Eliot. At least, the Eliot she'd known. First the decaf coffee, and now this. Could things really have changed so drastically over the past six years?

"How could you even think of giving up medicine? You're so talented." But at her words, his face became a familiar emotional wall, the classic expression Eliot wore whenever he would refuse to discuss a subject further. Clearly, the idea of giving up medicine was fraught with emotion for him. How could it not be? He'd never wanted anything more than to become a doctor. He obviously needed to talk about it. Which made it just as obvious that he never would.

"I'm not the only one who's changed. I never would have thought to see you working as a midwife."

She couldn't be sure, but she thought there might be a note of admiration in his voice. "Is it really that unexpected?"

"Don't get me wrong—you clearly have a knack for it. I'm very impressed by what I've seen so far." She tried to suppress the warm glow that rose within her at his praise. What Eliot thought of her shouldn't matter—or at least, it shouldn't matter *this much.* It was always nice to hear positive feedback from a doctor, but her heart rate was increasing just a little too quickly after Eliot's compliment.

But his next words felt as though he'd poured cold water over her. "I always thought that if you decided to work, you'd end up in some puff position at one of your father's companies."

"Excuse me?"

"You know—that your father would put you

in some meaningless role where you could stay out of the way until you got tired of having a job. It's impressive that you chose midwifery instead. It's a career with meaning and purpose."

His condescension was a slap in the face. "Is that what you thought of me?"

"Don't get mad. I'm trying to pay you a compliment."

"It's a hell of a backhanded compliment. You honestly thought I'd be satisfied to stay in some useless position my father arranged for me until I got 'tired' of having a job? Is that where you saw my life going when we were together?"

He grew defensive. "Tell me I'm wrong. Tell me that if you'd asked your father for a job six years ago, or today, or tomorrow, that he wouldn't set you up somewhere with a decent salary doing something that wouldn't get in the way of all the people at the company who do the real work."

Her father had, in fact, done exactly that for both of her sisters when they'd toyed with the idea of working. But that had never been what she'd wanted for herself. Eliot might be right about her father, and her situation, but he wasn't right about her.

"I wouldn't know," she snapped at him. "I

told you, I haven't spoken to my father in years. We're very different people."

"Are you," he said. It didn't sound like a question.

She knew his reaction was fair considering how she'd broken things off between them, but she also knew it was wrong. She felt all the animosity of their final fight rising up between them again. The expression on his face was an exact replica of the one he'd worn six years ago, when he'd accused her of being a spoiled princess and she'd said that he'd never even tried to understand her if he thought that and that he didn't know her at all. He'd agreed and stormed out moments later. He looked as though he might storm away now, and it made her heart ache, because she'd never meant to hurt him so badly.

But she also resented his perception of her as sheltered, inexperienced and spoiled. She hoped that wasn't the view he held of her today, but it was awful to think that he'd ever felt that way about her at all.

More than anything, she hated that her attempt to extend an overture of peace to Eliot had turned into a moment that brought them right back to where they'd ended things six years ago. They'd both changed. She knew that.

So why had her attempt at a friendly conversation turned sour so quickly?

"It looks like we're back where we started," he said, echoing her thoughts.

"Wait." She shook her head. "You're not wrong about my father. I could have done exactly what you said. Gotten some job that meant nothing, whenever I wanted. Left it whenever I wanted. And my father would have been happy to arrange it for me, because it would have kept me firmly under his control. But that wasn't what I wanted for myself. That's why I don't speak with him anymore. Because relying on him nearly cost me everything. My independence, my identity. Relationships that were important to me. He has a way of making everything impossible."

It was as close as she'd ever come to telling him that her father had forced her to break up with Eliot. It had been no secret that her father was against their relationship. But she'd always sworn to Eliot that she'd initiated the breakup under her own volition.

But to her utter surprise, he laughed. "In other words, you broke off contact with your father because he was too controlling."

"Yes. Why is that funny?"

"Because it's exactly why our relationship didn't work! You say that relying on your father nearly cost you your independence and your identity. Don't you realize that the exact same thing almost happened to me when we were together?"

She was absolutely aghast. "How can you say that? I would never, ever have used my money to control you, or anyone else, the way my father did."

"No, but you still went ahead and made all of the decisions in our relationship. You were the one who decided whether we stayed out or went in, whether we went to a restaurant or ordered pizza, even what kind of clothes I wore. Because it was your money."

His interpretation of their relationship felt completely unfair to her. She remembered the moments he was describing, but in a completely different way. It had been a joy for her to take Eliot places he'd never ordinarily been able to afford, and she'd bought him clothes because she'd known how much he wanted to fit in with his medical school colleagues—*he* was the one who'd said he felt uncomfortable wearing patched trousers and shirts that had withstood a thousand washings. She'd never meant for those gifts to express anything but love for him.

"As far as I was concerned, we were in an equal partnership."

"We were. But you were the one who decided how equal we'd be. You were the one who decided that I was good enough for you, not the other way around."

"I never felt that way. Not once."

"But that was how other people saw it."

"Who cares about what other people thought?"

"That's the point. You never had to care about that. But I did, because I was the one who was the cleaning lady's son. I was the one people were looking at, wondering how someone like me got to be with someone like you."

His words stung. She'd always known, during their relationship, that he was insecure about money, but she'd never realized his feelings ran so deep. Had he really felt so controlled by her? Had her privilege left her so totally blinded to his unhappiness over their inequalities? She'd been determined that his lack of money wouldn't matter to her. But it seemed to have mattered to him more than she'd ever understood at the time.

Even so. Eliot had never told her how he felt. Not like this. He might claim now that he'd tried, but she remembered things very differently. The lack of vulnerability, the guardedness. The shutting down whenever she tried to find clues that would help her discover his feelings. How could she have known how he felt unless he talked to her?

"You could have let me know that you felt this way," she said. "Even afterward."

"What was the point of talking about it? It wouldn't have changed anything. I thought the best thing for both of us was to move on."

"Moving on hasn't exactly been an easy road for me." She barely tried to mask the raw hurt in her voice. After all, he didn't know why she'd had to break up with him, did he?

"I'm sorry."

"Don't be. I'm…used to making mistakes in relationships."

"Well. You know what they say about mistakes. Everybody makes them. You, me…everybody."

And that, she thought, might be the closest either of them would ever be able to come to acknowledging that they'd made mistakes with one another. It certainly wasn't enough to heal the hurt that had happened between them. But it might be enough to lay the groundwork for something else.

As hard as it had been to hear how Eliot had felt—and she was going to need to think about it before she accepted his interpretation of their relationship—their conversation had also helped her understand a little more of what things had been like for him. If only he had told her all this sooner, she might not have hurt him so badly when she'd ended things. As it was, she'd inadvertently struck a blow exactly where it had wounded him the most.

But he was telling her now. If he could change, maybe their relationship could, too.

"It's been six years, Eliot. I know the idea of the two of us being friends is a long shot. Probably impossible. But we're the only two people on earth who really know what we've put one another through. If we can't be friends, then how about establishing a truce?"

He considered this. "I suppose stranger things have happened."

"Like me becoming a midwife? And you becoming a venture capitalist?"

"Exactly. If all that's possible...then maybe a truce is possible for us."

Bria was just beginning to feel a sense of relief when he added, "Besides, I'm only here for a short time, and then I'll be gone for good. What's the harm in two colleagues trying to get along with one another for just a few weeks?"

He was right. There shouldn't be any difficulty in the two of them trying to get along. In less than a month and a half, he would be gone from her life again.

And this time, when he left, he would be gone forever.

CHAPTER FOUR

"ONE MORE TIME, people! From the top!" Eliot clapped his hands, the signal for everyone to resume their places.

Bria paused for a moment to catch her breath. The maternal-fetal medicine team at St. Raymond's was running drills to prepare for the birth of Sandra Patterson's quintuplets. Multiple births were always complicated, and with quints, prematurity was a given. Some of the babies might weigh as little as two pounds. There were a host of other issues that could arise. Seconds would matter in ensuring that each of the five newborns was appropriately monitored during the first few moments after birth, especially since the quintuplets born last would be the weakest and in need of the most care. A smooth and speedy delivery could have significant long-term effects on each quint's quality of life. In the face of the unknown, Eliot wanted to be ready for anything, and as interim chief of obstetrics, he wanted the hospital staff to be ready along with him.

Bria returned to her place on the "baby assembly line" Eliot had designed, which was comprised of Eliot as the delivering physician, Caleb as the assisting surgeon and Hazel and herself as Sandra's midwives. Sandra herself was also there, as Eliot thought having her present during rehearsals might reduce her anxiety and help her to feel more relaxed once labor started. Bria approved wholeheartedly of Eliot's decision to include Sandra; many doctors didn't give much thought to the mother's emotional experience during birth, nor to the impact that fear and worry during delivery could have on later postpartum depression.

Though not everyone was quite as appreciative of Eliot's meticulous attention to detail. Hazel blew her bangs upward with an annoyed puff of air and leaned toward Bria. "If he says 'one more time' one more time, I'm going to start doubting his sincerity."

Bria smiled. "He's just being thorough."

And perhaps also a bit competitive. Eliot had told her that he'd learned of a hospital in Utah that had delivered quintuplets in five minutes. Five babies born in five minutes was an impressive feat, but Bria had a feeling Eliot was aiming for four minutes and thirty seconds, a record that would probably stand for some time if he could manage to achieve it.

At the moment, the team was clocking in at about eight minutes, although that was to be expected, as they were still discovering and working out new obstacles to plan around.

"Less chatter, more focus!" Eliot called out.

Eliot had turned the operating room into a miniature NICU. He'd requisitioned five of every item a newborn could possibly need: cooling blankets, bassinets, cardiopulmonary monitors, central lines, all color coded and labeled with letters from A to E for each baby. Bria could tell that when the day finally came for Sandra to deliver, things would run as close to clockwork as they could get.

The team ran through the drill twice more before Eliot allowed them to break for lunch. "You seem pleased," she told him. "We got that last one down to six minutes and thirty seconds."

She recognized the competitive gleam in his eye. "We're getting there. There's still lots of room for improvement." He noticed that Sandra was listening and was quick to reassure her. "I hope all of this preparation isn't worrying you, Mrs. Patterson. We just want you to have the smoothest delivery possible."

"You don't have to convince me that faster is better," said Sandra. "I'll just be glad to be on the other side of this." She shook her head in awe at the complex operations of the staff. "And to think that when I first got pregnant, I wanted a natural birth at home. Something quiet and low-key. Of course, at the time I didn't know I'd be giving birth to five."

"You've been doing incredibly well," Eliot replied. "But while you're here, I do think it's time for us all to talk about when to expect the big day. Right now you're at twenty-nine weeks gestation, which is great for quintuplets. But I'd like to do everything we can to get you to thirty-four weeks. And with plenty of bed rest and good care, I think we can do it."

Sandra hesitated. "Lots of bed rest, you say?"

"It's essential that you stay home in bed as much as possible."

Sandra looked as though she might cry. "I hear you, Doctor, and I want to give my little ones their best chance. But I've had so much bed rest already. I only leave the house once a week as it is, for my acupuncture and massage sessions at the Women's Health Center, and I think I'd go mad if I didn't have that." A tear rolled down her cheek, which she wiped away. "I'm sorry. It's all these hormones."

Bria took her hand. "None of this is what you expected, is it? Five babies, and now a C-section, and a huge team of doctors instead of the quiet birth at home that you wanted."

"I know I'm being ridiculous. All I really want is for the babies to be healthy. And I know you're all trying to do the best for our family. But I feel as though my life is about to be nothing *but* babies for quite some time."

Bria thought for a moment. "How about this, Sandra? I can talk to our acupuncturist and massage therapist about doing some home visits, so you don't have to come to the center."

"Could you really? It would mean so much to me." Sandra gave her a relieved smile. "That center is such a treasure."

As Bria fell into line to take a sandwich from the lunch table in the hallway, Eliot came to stand beside her. "That was quick thinking with Mrs. Patterson," he murmured. "I was about to give her a lecture on the importance of bed rest, but you were far more helpful."

"She just needs something to help her feel special," Bria replied. "Emotional health is as important as physical health, and bed rest is difficult."

"It's a good thing your massage therapist and acupuncturist make house calls."

"They normally don't," Bria replied. "But they make exceptions for special cases, and Sandra is definitely a special case."

Eliot gave her an odd look, as though he was studying her. "You really care about her."

"Of course I do," she said, surprised. "She's my patient."

"It's not just that, though. You care about how she's feeling, whether she's happy or upset. It matters to you."

"Of course it does," she said again. "What kind of midwife would I be if I didn't care how my patients were feeling?"

He didn't respond immediately but continued looking at her as though in a new light. "You don't seem as fazed by the pressure of these drills as anyone else."

She felt that same mixture of frustration and pleasure and annoyance that seemed to come up whenever he paid her a compliment. She was pleased to hear him say it, frustrated with herself for feeling pleased and annoyed with him for seeming so surprised at her competence. But she decided that if they were going to have a truce, she might as well fill in some of the blanks about her life. "I spent two years with an international health organization in Haiti before moving back to Portland," she said. "After a few years of delivering babies with scant medical resources, prepping for quintuplets in a hospital is a walk in the park."

She could tell he was surprised, but all he said was "Well, your experience shows."

It was the first positive thing he'd said about her that didn't feel completely backhanded. For once, she didn't feel plagued by the frustration that so often accompanied his feedback when they worked together.

But before she could say anything in response, Eliot was calling the team to attention again, announcing that he wanted to run the drill three more times before the end of the shift.

By the end of the day, Bria was surprised by how cohesive the teamwork felt. She, Hazel and Caleb had all worked together before, but Eliot seemed to fit right in. He had a way of recognizing everyone's talents, bringing the team together to work as a unit. As the day went on, they developed an easy flow, so that their work felt automatic, seamless.

She'd always known he would be an excellent doctor, and it was rewarding to see him in action. Bria could see the team's confidence in him growing with each new decision he made, and she couldn't help feeling a small amount of pride, because she'd been there at the beginning, when Eliot was working so hard to make his dream come true.

It tore at her heart to think that her father had almost interfered with that dream. Watching him work now, she could tell that the hunch she'd had years ago had been right: he belonged in a hospital. He was perfectly in his element, master of all, mindful of everything from his patient's needs to how the hospital system could help or hinder a complicated delivery.

She'd seen many doctors during her career, some who were talented and others who held no passion for their work. She could tell that Eliot was born to be a physician. It was almost worth all the sacrifice and heartbreak that had brought them here, just so she could have a chance to see him in action. He'd become the doctor he'd set out to be, even though there had been so much in his way.

She couldn't believe he was thinking of giving up medicine. He was so obviously talented. Would he really give up a career that was such an important part of his identity—for money? If he'd been as successful in business as he'd said, did he really need any more of it?

A pang of guilt followed. She'd been the one to tell Eliot that he wasn't good enough for her, that he couldn't provide the life she wanted. She'd been lying, of course. To protect him. But no matter what her motivations had been, Eliot had heard from her, someone he loved and thought he could trust, that he didn't have enough money. And now she knew he'd heard that throughout his childhood, as well, from people so shallow that it shouldn't matter what they thought. For days, she'd been remembering their conversation in the commissary, when he'd revealed how he'd felt about the financial inequality in their relationship. She'd never known that he'd felt as though her money gave her the lead when they were dating. Was that what was driving him to consider giving up a career in which he was so obviously gifted?

Eliot's voice called her attention back to the drill. "We're doing great, but I want to have one more day of practice before the big day. We're just above five minutes. Let's see if we can shave another thirty seconds off our time. In the meantime, everyone on the quintuplet team needs to keep their pager on them at all times. Remember, the message is QUINTS911. That message means to report here, to this delivery room, no matter what you're in the middle of. And don't forget…this is supposed to be fun."

Everyone laughed, and Bria thought again of how skilled Eliot was. It wasn't just his medical knowledge. He put everyone at ease, patients and medical staff included. She'd even noticed it in herself after only a day of working with him. Before, she'd been excited for Sandra, but now it was more. Now she felt excited for herself, too. Delivering quints was a momentous occasion, and she couldn't imagine anything more exciting than the delivery of five healthy babies at once.

And as she watched Eliot, she knew he felt it, too. His passion and excitement were apparent in his voice, his tone, his energy, and all of it was infectious.

How could he even think of quitting medicine?

Eliot couldn't wait to get out of his scrubs and into his hiking gear.

One of the few things he'd missed about Portland was the greenery. When it came to finding good hiking spots, Portland was full of gems. He remembered numerous hidden trails and waterfalls from his youth. He hadn't been to the city in such a long time that each excursion to a trail remembered from his childhood held fresh excitement, as he was able to enjoy the natural beauty with fresh eyes. He got all the joy of being a tourist while holding all the secret knowledge of a local. And even though his financial situation had improved considerably from his childhood, he still found simple pleasures such as hiking to be the most restorative after a long day.

Running the quintuplet drills had left him excited and nervous. He'd only delivered quints once before, during his residency, and then he'd mostly been observing. This time, he'd be in charge, and he was feeling all the weight of his responsibility.

He'd always felt there was nothing better than a hike in the woods to clear his mind and help him feel refreshed. He changed his clothes in the hospital's staff locker room and began walking toward Forest Park.

It was encouraging to see how the quintuplet team was coming along. He thought he'd chosen the team wisely, as everyone seemed to work well together, but he couldn't help noticing that he and Bria, especially, seemed to have a special kind of flow. The moment he thought of something, she already seemed to have anticipated his needs. He'd noticed that Hazel and Caleb, and in fact all the other members of the medical team, were often talking. That was good; everyone should be communicating with one another. But between him and Bria, it felt as though they didn't need to speak.

Perhaps it meant nothing. Or perhaps he was even imagining it. It would, he admitted to himself, probably feel nice to think that he and Bria shared some special understanding, after all the misunderstandings that had passed between them. When they'd spoken a few days ago, they'd argued and aired some past hurts, but things had been far calmer between the two of them since then. As though they were able to see each other more accurately now, after six years apart. He'd even noticed himself looking forward to when he and Bria could work together, which was a nice change from when he'd dreaded those moments.

It had felt good to be honest with her after all this time. So good, in fact, that he had to admit she had a point about his lack of vulnerability. He'd spent years hiding his feelings. That had been his go-to strategy for surviving high school. And later, in medical school, it had been the same. He started to form a list in his mind of the people he'd ever felt really comfortable opening up to. There was Caleb, to a certain extent. His mother…but he couldn't even tell her everything. Bria's name had been on the list once, but now it was mentally crossed out.

When he'd first come back to Portland, he'd been afraid that telling Bria how he really felt would only cause more conflict between them. Now it seemed to have actually brought them closer together.

Bria was certainly full of surprises. He'd been shocked when she told him she'd worked in Haiti for two years. He wondered what service organization she'd gone with. If she'd been gone for that long, it explained a lot: why there was barely any recent information about her online, the way she was so steady in a crisis, as well as her overall skill as a midwife. If she'd had to practice without much modern equipment or medicine, it probably was a luxury to have the resources of St. Raymond's available.

Something had changed as he'd seen her interacting with Sandra Patterson. She'd been so compassionate, so empathetic. He knew what it was. He'd seen it before, among the medical colleagues he had who were among the very best. Bria's care for her patients was real.

He'd worked with plenty of colleagues who were good at their jobs, but he could always tell when a medical professional really, truly cared about their patients as people. Bria had that ability. She had a passion for working with patients that he'd often felt, too. She was nothing like the overprivileged medical students he'd gone to school with, or the burned-out colleagues he'd met who could no longer muster empathy for their patients. Her feelings were genuine.

Careful, he thought. *You've been down this road before.*

He was all too aware that it wasn't safe to trust that Bria stood out, that she was different. And yet…he'd felt a burst of warmth for her when he'd seen her comforting her patient earlier. Something that went far beyond feeling impressed with a colleague's skill.

The feeling was so strong it was palpable, and it took him utterly by surprise.

He'd spent six years trying to put the past behind him. He'd met other women but had never seemed to be able to find what he was looking for. His wealth made it difficult to know if women were interested in him or in his checking account. After all his insecurity about Bria's fortune, and the difficulties he'd faced growing up in poverty, he was well aware of the irony of his own wealth interfering with his ability to have a relationship.

Seeing Bria again, hearing her laugh, smelling that vanilla-coffee scent that always lingered about her…all of it had awakened something within him that he thought had been dormant, maybe even gone forever.

He was almost to Forest Park. There were only a few hours of daylight left, so he intended to make a short hike up to the spot called the Witch's Castle. It was a popular hike for both residents and visitors, and so he supposed he shouldn't have been too surprised to hear a familiar voice.

"Eliot." Bria.

"Are you headed up to the Witch's Castle?"

"I go up there after busy workdays," she said.

"I guess great minds think alike. I was just about to head up there myself. It's one of my favorite hikes."

"I know. You were the first one to ever take me up there, remember?"

Now that she mentioned it, he did remember. They'd gone into the park with a picnic basket and had explored all the park's various treasures.

"I come here nearly every day," she continued. "It's one of the best places in the city to unwind."

He was touched that she'd continued walking here. It was as though she'd taken something good from the wreckage of their relationship.

But he was also uncomfortable with that line of thinking. He'd spent years trying not to think about Bria, and so the idea of her hiking along one of the same routes they used to travel together left him feeling unsettled. Had she thought about him as she walked here? Or had she simply enjoyed the trail with no associations to him? Either scenario threw his emotions into turmoil.

"I could take another trail, if you'd prefer," he said awkwardly.

She cocked her head to one side. "I thought we agreed to a truce."

"Still, if you're uncomfortable...or if you

want some peace and quiet, I can find some-where else to hike. It's a huge park. It's not as though I can't find another trail." His words were coming out a bit too fast.

She raised her eyebrows. "If *I'm* uncomfort-able? Is it possible, Eliot, that *you* might be the one who's uncomfortable? Or are you still not allowing yourself to have feelings?"

He stiffened, annoyed with himself for be-coming flustered and letting it show. "I'm not uncomfortable at all."

"Then let's get hiking. I'm sure we can han-dle being civil to one another even if we're not at work."

She fell into step beside him. Though her presence had disoriented him for a moment, he realized he was glad to have company. Even if it was Bria's company. Bria, who reminded him of bakery smells and leisurely mornings spent lingering over coffee. And the nights that had come before those mornings, when both of them had felt a heat so intense he'd once thought it would consume them both.

He wondered if she ever thought about those nights. Of course, he could never ask her. And she'd never shown any sign that the memories of their love life came to her mind the way they'd come to his from the moment his plane touched down in Portland. So there wasn't any point in thinking about them.

And yet, the memories of her arms reaching for him, her legs wrapped around him, had a way of gripping his mind at the most inopportune moments. Such as right now, for example.

He searched his mind for a topic that would get them as far from speaking of the past as possible. "I don't think the tour you gave me of the Women's Health Center did it justice," he said. "The more I hear about it, the more invaluable it seems to the community."

She frowned, as though she didn't want to talk about it right now. He couldn't believe it. He thought he'd chosen the exact subject she couldn't seem to talk enough about.

But then she sighed. "I might as well come clean. I didn't want to admit it to you during the tour, but the fact is, the center's in a pretty serious financial crisis."

"I'm sorry. I know it's important to you."

"It's all right. We're doing what we can to make up what we need with fund-raising. In fact, we've decided to organize a charity gala in a few weeks. I actually came out for a hike to avoid thinking about gala planning. Frankly, there are too many details and not enough time to sort them all out. But I don't want to let Hazel down. I promised her I'd take the lead, since I've done this kind of thing before."

"I remember." He'd always hated attending black-tie charity galas with Bria. He took no pleasure in wearing uncomfortable clothes to events where people wrote large checks to feel good about themselves while looking down their noses at him. "I thought you liked planning these kinds of things. You used to be able to throw them together in no time."

"That was when I wasn't working full-time as a midwife and managing a women's health center." She sighed again. "I really wasn't looking to take on a third job right now, but it can't be helped."

"Isn't there any way you could take more time? Reschedule it for next spring?"

"No. We need to act fast. We had a change with one of our major donors, which would have been fine, but then two others left as well. One passed away, one shifted funding to other causes... It's just a run of bad luck, all at once, and the financial consequences are going to hit us soon."

"So you need to get your fund-raising underway as soon as possible.

"Exactly. Hence, the gala. But there isn't a lot of time to plan. I don't even have anything to wear."

"What's wrong, you already wore each of your Oscar de la Renta gowns somewhere once?" He instantly felt ashamed of himself. He hadn't meant to be harsh. Bria was opening up, telling him about her life. He had no reason to goad her. But old habits died hard, it seemed, and so, he supposed, did old resentments. Still. He and Bria had agreed to a truce, and he needed to respect that if they were going to get through the next few weeks.

She narrowed her eyes at him and looked as though she was about to say something sharp in reply, but then her face softened. "I sold most of my clothes to a consignment shop a few years ago."

He was taken aback. "Why?"

"I was about to start work in Haiti, and I didn't see myself having much use for designer eveningwear ever again."

"But why sell them? Why not just…put them in storage, or something?"

She shrugged. "Because I needed the money."

"What?"

She bit her lip and then said, "I haven't taken any of my family's money in years. My father is leaving everything to my sisters."

His jaw dropped. "Why?"

"I've told you, because my father sees money as a way to control people. There are always strings attached, no matter what he says. And because as long as I knew I had the safety net of being dependent on him, I would never push myself to stand on my own two feet."

"And that was important to you."

"You have no idea how much. I wanted to be sure that I was making my own decisions, without being influenced by anyone else ever again."

A mix of emotions threatened to overtake him. Part of him was horrified at the idea of her walking away from such a fortune, yet he also felt a deep respect at her ability to stand up for her principles.

He didn't want to think about what her decision might mean regarding their past, but his mind raced on regardless of his desire. Was she implying that she had been influenced by her father to break up with him all those years ago?

The hope was irresistible, but along with hope came pain. Even if her father had swayed her, she was still the one who'd said they couldn't be together. Ultimately, she hadn't wanted to marry him. No matter what her motivations had been, nothing could change the past six years, and he refused to torture himself by getting mired in what-ifs.

"So you walked away from him."

"It's what had to be done. I was never going

to have my own life as long as I was in the shadow of his."

"So that's why the center is so important to you. That's why you got so mad when I assumed your father was responsible for all of it."

She nodded. "The center is entirely mine and Hazel's. It's why the gala has to be a success."

"Is there anything I can do to help?"

"How could you help?"

He felt his old insecurity tugging at him, looking for the insult: How could *you* help? But all he could see was genuine curiosity on her face, and hope that he might have answers she hadn't considered.

"I run a holding company that buys and sells medical centers."

"Ugh. Please don't tell me that you buy family clinics and turn them into soulless conglomerates."

"Those soulless conglomerates are the reason family clinics can survive. My partners and I buy clinics that are struggling financially and make them part of profitable corporate chains. There are doctors who wouldn't be able to stay in business if it weren't for us."

"That may be, but it's not going to happen to the center. We're going to keep our independence and our identity."

"I can respect that, but given the issues you're

facing, it would make a lot of sense to consider selling to a conglomerate. You and Hazel could make a tidy profit and stay on as employees to direct the center. You'd have better name recognition as part of a national chain of clinics, so you could expand your reach and help more people. It's not the terrible thing you think it is."

"But you're describing the best-case scenario, with investors who really get what Hazel and I have created and wouldn't turn on us the moment they've bought us out. Where would I find a firm like that? What firm would even understand our situation?"

"How about mine?"

She gawked at him. "I don't know if you're joking, but just in case you're not, I can think of about a dozen problems with that."

"Such as?"

"For one thing, our past."

"This would be strictly business. You wouldn't even have to deal with me, just managers from my firm. I'd be back in Boston. To be honest, buying the center would be a profitable move for me. And the expense would be minimal."

"We need to raise four hundred and thirty thousand dollars. That's minimal?"

"To me it is."

He watched her consider this. "For the record,

I'm serious about the offer. It would make a lot of sense for you to sell."

"No. It's my center, and I'm going to save it my way."

Even though he knew how she felt about the center, he'd thought she might jump at his offer to bail her out. The fact that she hadn't left him all the more impressed with her passion.

"Let me help you," he said again. When he saw she was about to protest, he quickly added, "I don't mean with money. Let me help you plan the gala. I can see how important the center's independence is to you, and I'll do everything I can to make the gala successful. But if it isn't… just know that you have another option."

"Why do you want to help?"

"Because I can."

As he'd amassed his fortune over the years, he had to admit that he'd occasionally thought about what might happen if Bria found out that he'd become wealthy. He wasn't above fantasizing about how it might feel to finally be the one offering Bria money, to show her that she needed him for a change. He knew it was petty, but he'd always thought there would be a kind of satisfaction in turning the tables on Bria.

But now, as he said the words, they had nothing to do with satisfaction. He wasn't offering to help her because he wanted to lord his wealth over her or make her feel small. He'd offered to help because he couldn't bear to think of that light of passion going out of her eyes if the center failed.

After a moment's pause, she said, "Eliot, are you a secret billionaire?"

The question was so unexpected that he couldn't help laughing.

"That's not the term I'd typically use, and *billionaire* is a stretch, but... I've done well for myself. Let's leave it at that."

"In that case, maybe you could help by inviting some of your rich investor friends from Boston to the gala."

"Consider it done. I'll give you a few more names for the mailing list. But make sure to tell them you're only interested in donations or they'll just want to buy the place."

They'd nearly reached the Witch's Castle, a stony structure covered by moss. The place had an aura of magic that gave even greater weight to its name. The air, normally filled with the chatter of other hikers, had grown quiet around them.

"I've always loved this place," Bria said.

"Isn't the stone house supposed to have a bit of a ghost story?"

"I like to think of it as a love story. Sometime in the nineteenth century, Mortimer Stump fell in love with Anna, a local settler's oldest daughter. Only they couldn't be together, because…" She swallowed. "Because Anna's father didn't approve."

Eliot traced the graffiti someone had left on one of the stone walls. "As I recall, this story doesn't turn out too well for poor Mortimer."

"Well, it didn't turn out great for Anna's father, either. One of many reasons why people shouldn't thwart young love."

Now it was his turn to swallow. "They really shouldn't."

Bria clambered up the stone steps and sat atop the wall. Eliot, tired, stayed on the ground below her. "Careful," he told her. "It's slippery."

"Don't worry, I'm used to climbing around on these stones." But even as she spoke, her ankle twisted at an odd angle, and she lost her balance and slipped backward down several steps.

Eliot caught her before she could completely fall over, wrapping his arms around her.

Let go, he thought, once he was sure she was steady. But he found that he didn't want to.

He turned her so that she was facing him, and then, before he even realized what he was doing, he bent forward to kiss her. His lips sought hers, and as she put her hand to the back of his head to press him forward, he crushed his mouth against hers, all the yearning of their years apart taking shape in a single kiss. He was intoxicated by her taste—the familiar vanilla lip gloss, coffee and the third, indefinable element that he could only classify as *her*. It was a taste he hadn't known he was craving for six years, and yet now that he'd had it, his desperation for more only grew.

He might have gone on kissing her indefinitely—if another hiker hadn't come running up to them, panting.

"Please," the man yelled. "I need help." He seemed to be in his late thirties, rather out of shape and completely unaware that he was interrupting anything.

"It's my wife," he gasped. "I had to leave her alone—you're the first other hikers I've seen. Something's wrong. I think she needs a doctor."

CHAPTER FIVE

THE KISS STOPPED almost as quickly as it began, the moment melting away at the sudden interruption. Bria disentangled herself from Eliot's arms, her heart racing. But there was no time to sort out her emotions, as complicated as they were. The hiker was clearly in distress and desperate for help.

"Please," he gasped again. "I ran all the way here, and I've had to leave her alone."

"We're both medical professionals," said Eliot. "Tell us what's wrong, and we'll help in any way we can."

"Oh, thank god. She was stung by a bee, but for some reason she won't use her EpiPen."

"Can you take us to her?"

"Yes, she's just down the road. She couldn't walk anymore, and we both left our phones in the car. I shouldn't have left her, but I didn't know what else to do.

"You did exactly right," Eliot said as they followed the man back down the trail at a rapid pace.

Bria willed herself to snap back into medical mode. Though she tried to focus herself mentally, her emotions after that kiss ran the gamut from terrified to confused to pure, unadulterated joy.

You can sort out your feelings later, she told herself.

If she and Eliot were about to deal with a medical emergency, she needed to remain in the here and now.

"Up ahead," the man said.

A woman was sitting on the ground next to the trail, her head folded over bent knees. Three or four people hovered near her; it appeared as though another hiking group had come upon her while her husband had gone for help.

"Has anyone called for an ambulance?" Bria asked as they approached the woman. One of the hikers nodded and raised his phone.

"Excellent. Then the best thing you can all do is give this woman some space while my colleague and I take a look at her. Clear away, please. Unless you're a medic, I want everyone at least six feet back."

Bria knelt to take the woman's pulse, which was weak and erratic. Her neck and chest were covered in large hives, and her lips were swollen. "What are your names?" she asked the man.

"I'm Tim, and she's Rachel." He shook his head, his face distraught. "We're from Nevada. This trip was supposed to be a chance to recover after a rough year, and…" His voice faded, and Bria could see how frightened he was. "She has to be all right."

"We'll do everything we can. But I need you to stay focused while I ask you a few questions. Is there anything wrong with the EpiPen?"

He handed it to Bria. "It seems fine, as far as I can tell."

It seemed to be in good working order to Bria as well. "You said she was stung by a bee—does she have any other known allergens?"

"Not that I know of. She hasn't been stung since she was a child, but it must have been pretty bad back then, because she's always had her EpiPen with her whenever we go on hikes, just in case. I've never seen her like this before." His lower lip began to tremble, and he looked as though he might cry.

"Tim, I want you to talk to Dr. Wright while I see to Rachel. Tell him everything you might know about Rachel's medical history. I'll see if I can help her." She nodded to Eliot, who took the hint and steered Tim a few yards down the trail, out of hearing distance.

Bria noticed that the woman's breaths were coming in a strained wheeze. "Rachel, you're showing classic signs of anaphylaxis. Your husband said you got stung by a bee?"

Rachel nodded, but as she saw the EpiPen in Bria's hand, her eyes widened and she pushed Bria's arm away.

"Don't worry, I'm a nurse-midwife, and my friend over there is a doctor. I won't do anything you don't want me to. But I've taken your pulse, and your blood pressure seems dangerously low. The sooner I give you the shot, the better."

Rachel shook her head violently. She tried to speak, but her lips were too swollen. Tears of frustration formed at the corners of her eyes.

Bria looked over at Eliot and saw that he was on his phone. He saw her looking and called, "Ambulance here in ten."

Good. Bria put her hand on Rachel's shoulder. "Medics will be here soon. In the meantime, we do need to use your EpiPen to give you the best recovery."

Rachel shook her head again and craned her neck to look at where Tim and Eliot were standing. They were deep in conversation. She looked back at Bria, shook her head and patted her stomach.

"Oh! You're—

Before she could say the word *pregnant*, Rachel put a finger to her lips and shook her head again.

"I understand." Bria lowered her voice. "He doesn't know?"

Rachel shook her head again, tears falling more freely. She tried again to speak, but her breath was coming too hard and fast.

Bria had a feeling that Rachel's harsh breathing wasn't just due to anaphylaxis but to the woman's distress. She hastily fished her own phone out of her hiking bag and opened the text function. "Here, just type whatever you want to say on my phone." She handed it to Rachel.

Rachel hurriedly texted.

Had miscarriage last year. Didn't want to tell him like this.

A recent miscarriage—no wonder Rachel was so distraught. By the looks of things, Rachel was probably early in her first trimester; even a midwife wouldn't have guessed she was pregnant without looking carefully for the signs. And after her loss, Rachel was probably walking on eggshells out of fear of losing another chance at a baby.

"Don't worry. It's very early still, right? So you can probably use your EpiPen safely. There's no known risk to the baby." Rachel's eyes were wide, and Bria knew she wanted what every worried mother wanted: certainty that she was making the right decision, knowledge that her baby would be all right.

Her hunch was confirmed seconds later when Rachel texted another message on her phone.

Probably???

There had been so many times since she'd become a midwife that Bria had longed to give her patients certainty. But she'd learned very early on in her career that making false promises only made things worse. Unable to give Rachel the certainty she craved, Bria tried for the next best thing: honesty.

"I can't promise there's no risk at all. But I can guarantee that your anaphylaxis poses a greater risk to your baby right now than using your EpiPen."

Rachel's breathing grew more relaxed. Bria could see that she was thinking it over, trying to make the best decision in a crisis. Then she gripped Bria's hand and nodded, pulling up the hem of her hiking shorts. Bria pushed the tip of the EpiPen firmly against the side of Rachel's thigh.

The injection took effect within moments. Bria was relieved to see the hives disappearing from her chest and neck, and the swelling in her face began to recede. They sat together as Rachel's breathing eased.

Bria took her pulse again. "You should start feeling better soon. Your pulse is still a bit slow, though, and that's something we'll want to get back to normal right away, because if you have low blood pressure, that can have an effect on the baby. Dr. Wright said the ambulance should be here any minute, and they'll take you to the hospital to make sure you're all right. They'll probably want to keep you overnight just to be sure."

"A hospital," Rachel whispered, shaking her head. "Tim is going to freak."

"If you like, we can just say that a hospital stay is standard procedure and nothing more. I would recommend that you go to the hospital even if you weren't pregnant."

Rachel paused. "It was so hard when we lost the first baby. I was trying to wait for just the right time to tell him I was pregnant again. I know if I tell him now, after this emergency, he'll just worry nonstop."

"But you need support, too. I can tell you're tremendously concerned about your baby. That's why you wouldn't let me give you that EpiPen."

Rachel gave a husky laugh, her voice still

weak. "That was stupid. I panicked. I didn't know what to do."

"Not stupid at all. You were desperate to do the best thing for your baby. It's hard to make those kinds of decisions under pressure, when you don't have all the information. You didn't know if the EpiPen was safe. And anaphylaxis is sudden and frightening. Considering the circumstances, I think you did well. You waited for a medical professional to arrive, and you trusted their opinion."

Rachel gave her a watery smile. "I'm just lucky you were here."

"I'm glad I was, too. But think about the support you already have. The longer you keep this a secret, the more you're cutting yourself off from someone who could help."

"I know. Tim wouldn't want me to feel alone. It's just that we've wanted a child for so long. I can't stand to think of losing another one. And Tim would be devastated, too."

Though she'd never shared Rachel's experience, Bria could understand how she felt. It must have been devastating for Rachel to have her hopes raised and then dashed. No wonder she'd been afraid to use the EpiPen.

She gave Rachel's hand a squeeze. "Part of protecting your baby is about keeping you as healthy as possible. And that means having

Tim's support as well." She retrieved a business card from her pocket and handed it to Rachel. "When you're ready, why don't you call the Multnomah Falls Women's Health Center? We have therapists who work with couples who've faced miscarriage, and they can give you some guidance on how to find a good counselor at home in Nevada."

The ambulance arrived, sirens blaring, and Bria returned to Eliot.

"Let's give Tim and Rachel some privacy," she replied, steering him away from where the couple sat by the roadside. They walked a little farther down the road and then heard Tim give a shout of joy. Bria turned to see him throwing his arms around Rachel.

"Well, it looks like she told him."

"Told him what?"

"That she's pregnant."

"Ah, so that's why you took over so quickly back there, leaving me to tend to the husband."

"I thought I might be able to find out why she was refusing the EpiPen more quickly without her husband around. Anyway, we aren't at the hospital now. You don't get to pull rank out here."

"So it seems. Perhaps I should refer to you as Dr. Thomas from now on."

"Hmm, that does have a nice ring to it."

"You did very well. You had her calmed so quickly. I might have just given her the injection right away, but your approach was better—asking her questions, explaining things, calming her down. Patients always do better when they understand the treatment."

Her heart warmed at the compliment, even though she'd been trying to tell herself since he'd arrived that his opinion didn't matter. And then she remembered.

You kissed him.

The medical emergency had absorbed her so much that she hadn't even had time to think about it.

What on earth had happened back there at the Witch's House?

He seemed pretty eager to kiss you, too.

It had been an accident, falling into his arms like that. But what had happened afterward had been more than an accident. She could have pushed away from him instead of allowing herself to melt into his arms. Instead of leaning her face closer to his.

She realized he'd been silent for a few moments and wondered if he was thinking of their kiss, too.

"That was pretty close back there," he said. Her heart nearly stopped.

"But I supposed it's for the best, if it means the secret's out," he continued.

"The secret?" Her lips were dry.

"At least now that he knows she's pregnant, she won't have to bear all that worry alone."

Of course. His mind was still with their patients. She was glad the growing darkness hid the blush on her cheeks.

"That's the thing about secrets," she said, searching desperately for something to say that wouldn't show him her mind had been occupied with entirely different thoughts. "It always feels better once they're out."

She'd been trying to steer away from the subject of the kiss, but somehow it seemed as though they were right back where they'd started.

They had, in fact, reached the beginning of the trailhead, where they'd begun the evening's adventures.

"Well, that was unexpected," she said, trying to keep her voice bright and casual. "We both came here looking to relax, but duty called instead."

"Ninety percent of being in the medical profession is about being in the right place at the right time. I'm just glad we both decided to come here tonight."

"Me, too. I'm so happy we were able to help in time."

He reached out as though to put a hand on her shoulder, but then his hand trailed all the way down her arm, finally clasping her hand. She shivered under his touch.

"I meant for other reasons as well."

Oh. Alarm bells rang within her ears. His hand still held hers. The pull toward him was magnetic, irresistible. She should tell him good night. She should remind him that they were friends and colleagues, and that trying to be anything more would only lead to both of them getting hurt all over again.

She opened her mouth to say all those things, but what came out instead was "Would you like to come over to my place?"

Bria didn't live far from Forest Park. Dusk was falling as they walked, and she found herself once again relieved that the growing darkness hid her expression. She'd never been very good at hiding her feelings. She was sure she looked as nervous as she felt.

Eliot, on the other hand, was his typical stoic self. It was hard to make out his face in the darkness, but even if she could, she wasn't sure she would have found much there to inform her as to what he was feeling.

If she hadn't been emboldened by their kiss, she probably would have listened to the part of her that had better sense, and they'd have parted back at the trailhead. But she could still feel her lips tingling. Could still feel the way his arms had wrapped around her, holding her as though he'd never let her go.

But we did let go of each other.

Once. A long time ago. No matter what happened next, she couldn't let herself forget that. Becoming involved with Eliot was almost a certain road to heartbreak.

But what if their involvement was for one night only?

There was so much that was unresolved between them. Their relationship was such a tangle that she didn't think it could ever be sorted out.

But maybe they didn't need to sort it out. Maybe they could be together, just for now, and get whatever resolution the night could afford them.

They reached her building, an older brownstone with creaking front steps. She unlocked the main door and led him up to her hallway.

"One second," she said when they reached the door. She slipped into her apartment, a modest one-bedroom, and flicked the lights on. Her housekeeping skills were relaxed at best, but work had called her away from home so often recently that she hadn't been home much, which meant that things were relatively neat. *Relatively* being the key word.

She dashed into her bedroom. Within twenty seconds, she had kicked a pair of old jeans underneath the bed, cleared a plate peppered with toast crumbs from her nightstand and turned the stuffed panda from her childhood to face the wall. Perfect. She returned to the doorway, where Eliot stood. Waiting.

"Come on in," she said, trying to calm her fluttering nerves.

He entered, and she instantly became nervous about what he might see when he looked around the apartment. Was there some clutter she'd forgotten to attend to?

But his eyes were fixed on her. They seemed to burn with a question. Eliot had always been had to read, but the intensity of his gaze left no room for wondering if he'd misread her intentions when she'd invited him here.

He stepped toward her, and she didn't back away.

He put his hands on her shoulders lightly and traced his hands all the way down her arms, just as he had in the park. This time, she didn't try to hide her shiver. He bent his head down until his lips just barely grazed hers. Unable to wait any longer, she pressed her mouth against his. His kisses were soft and slow, as though after all these years, he wanted to take his time in rediscovering her. His tongue entered her mouth, and a slow urgency began to build between them. He pulled her body closer, and she leaned into him, feeling herself melt against him.

He rubbed his hands along her back, her waist, as though he was exploring her body for the first time. And yet, when he reached one breast, he paused there, stroking her nipple between his thumb and forefinger. Clearly, there were some things he hadn't forgotten.

She arched her back, reveling in his touch, aching to feel his hands on her bare skin. Anticipating her desire, he began to unbutton her blouse, slipping it from her shoulders as though he'd unwrapped a present. With a flick of his fingers, he undid her bra, which fell to the floor in a crumple of black lace. He bent his head to give her breasts their due attention, his tongue attending to all the old places—and some new ones as well.

"Come over here," she whispered, tearing herself away before she became lost in sensation. She took his hand and led him to the bedroom. He kicked off his shoes, and she began undoing his belt buckle as he pulled off his T-shirt over his head to reveal the smooth planes of his body. She unbuttoned her own trousers, and he slipped them off along with her underwear in one smooth motion.

She stood before him, naked. For the first time in six years.

She felt self-conscious, but at least he was naked, too. He still seemed as perfect as she remembered. His thighs were long and lean, his abdomen well-defined. As he gazed at her, she saw him growing hard, and she knew she wasn't the only one whose need was becoming urgent.

He drew her close and muttered something in her ear. Caught up as she was in the thrill of feeling his bare skin against hers, it took her a moment to realize he was asking about protection. She reached into the nightstand, where she had an endless supply of condoms, not because she had need of them often, but because such were the perks of working in women's health care.

He laid her on the bed and took her mouth with his, both of them releasing themselves to the desire that overtook them. Her thoughts melted away as she became lost in the sensation of his body atop hers, her limbs intertwining with his.

His hands moved down to caress the space between her legs, and the need within her became a fire that she was unable to control. She writhed under him and gasped his name to let him know she wouldn't be able to hold on much longer.

He shifted his hips, and she could feel him, hard and hot against her. As she tilted her hips upward to meet his, he entered with a long, slow thrust that made her moan with pleasure.

He moved within her, slowly at first, and then his pace quickened as she joined him, their bodies coming together in a rhythmic dance that they knew of old, yet that still somehow felt brand-new. She arched beneath him, and he thrust until she was teetering on the edge of ecstasy.

Finally, she let herself go. She heard his groan as though from a great distance, heard him calling out her name. She felt the sensation of stars bursting inside her over and over again. Finally, her body collapsed against his, sated and replete. An empty place within her, one that she'd denied even to herself for so long, had been filled at last.

Stars, she thought, barely able to form thoughts in her mind. Her last thought, before her eyes closed, was that she hadn't been aware of wishing on one. But if she had, she would have wished for this.

The first rays of morning light made their way through Bria's window. She blinked her eyes open and saw that Eliot was still there, his eyes shut, his face in peaceful repose. She'd forgotten those gentle snores of his: quiet enough to let her sleep, but just loud enough to make her feel his comforting presence. She snuggled closer to him, allowing herself to inhale the faint cinnamon spice scent that always lingered on his skin.

She couldn't remember the last time she'd had sex that had left her feeling so satisfied, so complete. The few encounters she'd had, scattered over the last six years, hadn't held much significance for her. She'd been seeking something, and after failing to find it for so long, she hadn't merely decided it didn't exist—she'd forgotten that she'd ever hoped for it in the first place.

But last night had awakened that forgotten part of her. She'd given in to her feelings and her memories, allowing the two of them to return to the past for one fleeting, shining moment.

Of course, their future remained to be determined. Eliot shifted in the bed. One of her rumpled sheets nearly slid off him, not leaving much to the imagination. She relaxed her body against his. She refused to spoil this moment by worrying about the future when she had such a scene of actual perfection in front of her right now.

He stretched and rolled over to face her, batting his eyes open. He saw that she was awake and smiled.

"Are you cold?" she asked. "I can grab another blanket from the closet."

He put an arm around her waist and pulled her even closer to him. "I've got everything I need to keep me warm right here." She nestled against his chest, indulging in the hypnotic rhythm of his heartbeat.

"Besides—" he kissed the top of her head "—you've got the heat blasting away."

"That's radiator heat for you. I can't control it." The only buildings in which she'd been able to afford the rent for a one-bedroom apartment had been more than a hundred years old. Central air was one of the luxuries she sorely missed from her past life. Her inefficient radiator meant that she rarely slept with blankets and often wore shorts and tank tops when home alone, even in the winter. At least she was never cold.

His eyes wandered around her apartment. It wasn't fancy, but it was cozy, and it was special, because it was hers. She'd found that she enjoyed decorating on a budget. Her room might not look as stately as it had when she'd lived in her father's mansion, but each item had personal meaning to her. She noticed him taking in the wall hangings, the collage of photographs artfully displayed on her bureau.

"I like your place. It's a fantastic location, and even though it's small, it feels homey."

"That's what I was going for."

"It must be a far cry from what you're used to, though."

She nodded. "I think this whole apartment could probably fit into one of my father's guest bathrooms."

"Was it hard to adjust, coming from a place like that to a place like this?"

"No. Not for a second." She saw his eyebrows lift, so she explained further. "After spending two years in Haiti, I understood how much everything was relative. My family's estate might be opulent compared to this apartment. But my apartment has everything I need. Warmth, a refrigerator, a solid roof. All I had to do to get comfortable was add a strong Wi-Fi signal and a decent coffee maker."

"What made you decide to go to Haiti?"

"I had just finished my nurse-midwife program. That was where I met Hazel. I was so impressed by how she knew exactly who she was. But I still didn't know myself at all. I needed a change, and that change needed to be something meaningful. Something that would show me who I wanted to be, rather than the person everyone thought I should be."

"And did it work? Did you find yourself?"

She thought for a moment. "I definitely found a new appreciation for different parts of my life.

Friendships became so much more valuable to me. Things I'd always took for granted, like electricity and clean drinking water, became small miracles to enjoy. I don't know if I exactly found myself, but I think I came to understand my own life far better than I used to."

"I think it would have been hard for a lot of people to give up so much."

She hesitated, and then admitted, "Full disclosure—my coffee maker is a Breville. I may have given up my family's fortune, but I didn't become a saint."

He buried his face in her hair and laughed. "I don't know what that is, but I assume you gave up as much as you could stand."

"Everybody has their limit."

"I'm not surprised at all to hear that the coffee maker is yours. Speaking of which. What are we going to do for breakfast?"

"Well…" She held the pause for as long as she could, not wanting to let the moment go. But she couldn't put it off any longer. Last night had been exquisite, but the sun was in the sky, and a new day had begun. They couldn't avoid talking about the night before without engaging in more denial than she could tolerate.

"Breakfast is a problem that's easily solved," she said. "But first, what are we going to do about last night?"

"Do we need to do anything about it?"

She'd been sitting up with the sheets around her, but at his words, she flopped backward into the bed with her hands over her eyes. This was exactly why she hadn't wanted to have this conversation. It was why she'd wanted to linger against his body, enjoying the cinnamon scent of him for as long as possible. Last night had been exciting, an unexpected opportunity to re-ignite the heat that had once existed between them. That clearly *still* existed between them.

But if she expected him to reveal any feelings about their night together, she was sorely mistaken. Mistaken, but not surprised. She knew Eliot. If she was going to get any feelings out of him, she'd have to go in with a pair of pliers.

Was he regretting last night? Did he feel it would create unnecessary complications, for them to be romantically involved while they were coworkers?

"We need to at least talk about it," she said. The room, which had seemed so warm just a moment ago, now felt tense and uncomfortable. She took a deep breath and decided to get things over with. Things between them were already complicated, and she would rather rip the bandage off all at once instead of allowing the two of them to labor under any further misunderstandings. "Do you have any regrets?"

"Absolutely not," he said, to her utter relief. "In fact, I'd be glad to repeat the experience as often as possible."

That was unexpected. She'd assumed he'd merely given in to physical attraction, just as she had. Her heart felt lighter than it had in years, and yet she cautioned herself, *be careful, go slow.* She'd need to make sure she understood his intentions perfectly before allowing her heart to soar even the slightest bit higher. "But you're leaving in a little over a month."

"Then what would you say to making the most of that month?"

Her heart no longer felt as though it was soaring. It was more like spinning, leaving her uncertain of her direction. She knew what he was about to suggest, and she saw the sense of it. Eliot's life was in Boston. Hers was in Portland.

"Are you suggesting what I think you're suggesting?"

He put an arm around her. "We obviously have an attraction to one another. Maybe we could enjoy the physical part of that attraction without the other complications that always get us into trouble. No romance. Just sex. And then at the end of it, we say our goodbyes."

She hesitated. A fling with Eliot. Part of her leaped at the idea; another part warned her that she was setting herself up for hurt. But how much could they really hurt each other in a month? And given their past, these might be the only terms on which they could realistically be together. Even after last night, her body craved closeness to his. He was right about their attraction to one another. After last night, there was no mistaking that. But she couldn't see how they could ever have anything more. She'd hurt him so badly in the past. How could he ever trust her with his heart again? She couldn't imagine it was possible.

If she was completely honest with herself, she'd been longing to touch him, to feel the heat of his skin against hers, from the moment he'd returned. Despite her best efforts, she hadn't been able to stop thinking about him, and she was beginning to doubt whether she ever would. A brief fling might be her only hope of ever getting over him, once and for all. It wasn't a re-kindling of their relationship. That could never happen. But it might be the next best thing—closure.

"Just one month, then?" she said, wanting to be absolutely clear.

"Just one month. No promises. No romantic involvement. We keep things purely physical. And then at the end of it, we say our goodbyes."

After all that had passed between them, did she really have anything to lose? Breaking up with him had been like having a piece of her heart torn out. But this would be different. This time, there would be no breakup, because there would be no relationship.

"All right. I'll agree on one condition."

He cocked an eyebrow at her. "What's that?"

She looked him in the eye. "That when you leave, we have a *real* goodbye. No taking off suddenly, without warning. When the time comes, I'll drive you to the airport, we'll hug and we'll have an actual goodbye instead of a painful one." Their last goodbye had been so harsh; they'd hurt each other so much. She wanted this chance for closure, for them both to be able to move on.

Last night had been about reminiscence, about connecting to the heat between them that had always made their relationship special. But she held no false hope that one night together had anything to do with their future. She'd killed any real feelings he might have had for her by breaking up with him, and by now they'd both built separate lives apart from each other. She wasn't so naive as to think that his desire for her was about anything more than being caught up in the moment and the memories between them. Allowing herself to want anything more than that would only result in getting hurt.

But she thought it was fair for her to want a

kinder farewell than they'd had six years ago. Maybe their month together could give them a chance to write over the pain of their last good-bye. It couldn't hurt to try.

"All right," he said. "I think I can offer you that."

"Great," she said, kissing him on the cheek. She extricated herself from the bedsheets. "Now, about that breakfast. Let me make you a cuppa, and then maybe you'll understand why I kept the fancy coffee machine."

She fixed their coffees the way they both liked them—his with a dash of cinnamon, hers with a scoop of cocoa. Even the smell brought a sense of nostalgia. She'd have to be cautious about getting swept up in that, though. Revisiting some memories might be fun, but she didn't want to get her heart broken all over again. All she wanted to do was enjoy the present moment, however fleeting it might be.

CHAPTER SIX

"IT SEEMS LIKE everyone on staff just loves you."

Eliot shrugged, but inwardly, he was pleased by Caleb's words. He hadn't seen much of his friend since he'd come to Portland, but Caleb had stopped by his office at St. Raymond's to see how he was enjoying being interim chair.

"*Love* is a strong word—I'm just glad to hear I'm fitting in. I appreciate the feedback, though. And the opportunity. I didn't realize just how much I've missed doing medicine full-time. Working at a hospital like this has been like stepping into another world, if only for a few weeks."

"It doesn't have to be just for a few weeks, you know. I've talked with Dr. Anderson. He'd be glad to end the search for a new hire now and keep you on permanently."

Eliot frowned, the old conflict welling within him. Caleb couldn't know just how tempted Eliot was to take him up on his offer. But the salary he'd make at St. Raymond's was barely a fraction of what he could make working at his firm in Boston. And the senior partners were counting on him to return. He couldn't simply walk away from his responsibilities.

But more importantly, there was the matter of Bria. He liked the way things had been between them since they'd established their arrangement of a purely physical, no-emotional-strings-attached affair. Their physical chemistry had always been good, and now it was exhilarating, perhaps because he'd been trying to ignore his attraction to her from the moment he arrived. But now he didn't need to hold back. They could both enjoy one another without having to worry about feelings from the past. Or any feelings at all, really. Emotional attachment made things far too complicated.

But if he stayed in Portland permanently, he risked deepening things with Bria. Even now, after only two weeks with her, he felt himself growing more involved. He'd noticed himself looking forward to spending time with her and feeling disappointed when she wasn't nearby. These were dangerous feelings. He couldn't allow himself to grow close to her again. He was enjoying their physical connection, but he had no interest in anything else. Especially not when the chances of having his heart shattered again were so high. The sooner he returned to Boston, the better.

"I'm afraid I have too many obligations in Boston," he told Caleb.

"Is that right? Because I was wondering if a certain midwife might be affecting your decision."

Eliot jerked his head up. "What do you mean?"

"I've been talking with Hazel, and she said you two have a history. I hope that hasn't created any problems. When I asked you to work here, I had no idea that you'd be in such close proximity to your ex. I'm sorry."

"Don't be. How could you have known? I never told you about her."

"Is there…anything you'd like to tell me about her now?"

"Why do you ask?"

"Because Hazel and I get the impression that whatever is between you two right now might be *more* than just history."

Eliot paused. He and Bria hadn't discussed how open they planned to be about their fling. But if she was talking to Hazel about it, then she couldn't fault him for saying anything to Caleb. "We've figured out an arrangement that works for both of us. But it won't complicate anything. We've both agreed, no talking about the past and no emotions."

"No, that definitely won't complicate anything," Caleb said dryly. "Those kinds of arrangements tend to work out really well."

"This one will," Eliot insisted. "It's not like other short-term relationships. We didn't just meet each other. We have a past. So we already know that getting emotionally involved is a mistake. We don't have to go through all that again. This is just about…moving on."

"Having sex with your ex is moving on? Eliot, you're one of the most brilliant people I know, so I'd never question your judgment. But doesn't getting involved with someone from your past feel more like moving backward than forward?"

"That's the beauty of it. We're not getting involved at all. This is more like a long goodbye."

Caleb shook his head. "Well, you're the medical and financial wizard. I'm just a lowly obstetrician. I won't presume to give you advice. But… I'm around if you want to talk, okay?"

He left Eliot to his work. But try as he might to focus on chart review, Eliot's mind kept swirling with questions.

Caleb's doubts about his arrangements with Bria could be easily dismissed. Eliot was perfectly satisfied with the ground rules of their affair. Caleb might not understand because he didn't know the full force of his attraction to Bria. And knowing that she was attracted to him, too, was like a drug he couldn't get enough of. But Eliot was certain that if he and Bria acted on their attraction, they could get one another out of their systems by the time he left. He'd be able to move on and finally find someone else, because he wouldn't be preoccupied with the way he felt about her any longer.

Caleb had also dropped something of a bombshell with his suggestion that Eliot might stay on at St. Raymond's permanently. Eliot had often thought about working full-time at a hospital, but only in an abstract sense. Caleb's suggestion had thrown his decision into stark reality. For the first time in a long time, Eliot wasn't sure what to do.

He felt more energized than he'd been in years. He'd meant it when he told Caleb that being at the hospital was like being in another world. One he hadn't realized how much he'd missed. Immersing himself in a medical environment offered a dramatic change from his career back in Boston. It was a change he had needed, badly.

His life in Boston had become rote, mechanical. But hospital work made him feel alive. Even days like today, which consisted mainly of signing off on charts and reviewing complex cases, left him feeling excited rather than worn-out. The cases piqued his interest and his curiosity.

Even the background conversation of the nurses and physician's assistants felt invigorating. Everything about the hospital made him look forward to coming to work in the morning.

At home, his business partners were constantly trying to convince him to give up his medical license so that he'd have more time to spend on his work. But here, he had colleagues nearby who understood and valued the satisfaction of a career as a physician.

His office door was open, and he happened to hear Bria's voice from down the hall. She was talking over a case with one of the nurses.

Everything about the hospital felt right to him, including working with her.

He'd been so afraid of running into her when he returned to Portland. But the moment he kissed her, all those fears had fallen away. Kissing her had felt like he was coming home again. And when they'd made love, it had felt as though he'd found where he belonged.

When they'd arranged their fling, he'd initially been concerned that there might be some awkwardness between them at work. But if anything, they worked even better as colleagues now. It felt as though their physical connection had somehow given them an understanding that needed no words.

Though all seemed well between them, there

was one small worry that had been nagging at the back of his mind ever since he and Bria had helped those hikers on the trail to the Witch's Castle. It had arisen after Bria's comment about secrets.

It always feels better once they're out.

He did have a secret, and it could make her feel differently about him. He'd realized he didn't want to tell her, but he knew it would only get worse the longer it remained unsaid.

He'd never told her about his mother's Christmas bonus, and the more he saw of her, the more certain he felt that she didn't know anything about it.

It wouldn't be that surprising if Calvin had never told her. The man had found it difficult enough to see his daughter as a person, let alone care about her feelings. The Thomas reputation was far more important to Calvin than any preferences of Bria's.

Would Bria feel any differently about him if she knew that his money essentially came from her father? She'd told him that it had been years since she'd lived off her family's trust. What would she think of him for having taken Calvin's money at such a critical time?

It was so important to her not to feel controlled by her father. Would she think less of him? Especially after she'd been able to step away from her family's wealth?

Even if she did, he didn't know what he could have done differently. He could never have stopped his mother from taking that money. It had meant too much to her, and she'd sacrificed too much for him. She'd been so proud to bestow it on him, believing that her years of work had finally enabled her to provide for him the way she'd always wanted. Not only was he not going to take that happiness from her, he'd fight anyone who did. But what if Bria saw it as a lie? What if she thought he'd deliberately been keeping this a secret from her?

And was it really a secret, or simply something he'd decided not to tell her? Was there even a difference?

He had a feeling Bria might think so.

But he didn't want to bring it up with her. And morally, he thought he would be in the clear even if he never told her. He and Bria had agreed that they weren't in a relationship. They'd probably never see each other after he returned to Boston. So telling her about the money would only risk upsetting her for no reason. After six years, there was no point in rehashing old history. He didn't want to spoil their time together by bringing up the past, and he didn't think she did, either.

* * *

Bria had been excited when Eliot asked if she'd wanted to meet for dinner after her shift. She was doing her best not to analyze the connection between them. For right now, she simply wanted to enjoy what they had together.

If she thought about it too much, she'd have to recall that Eliot was leaving his position at St. Raymond's soon. Which would mean that there was nothing keeping him in Portland. But she didn't want to dwell on those thoughts, because they interfered with what their time now was supposed to be about: tying up the loose ends of their relationship and saying goodbye in a kinder way than they'd been able to six years ago.

She was loving the sex, but even more than that, she'd been enjoying spending time with him outside work—and outside the bedroom. Though not all their excursions went as planned.

She poked at her duck confit, her stomach growling. "I didn't realize this was what you had in mind when you suggested we meet for dinner this evening."

She'd thought they might go out for something casual, but Eliot had surprised her with reservations at L'Epicure, one of Portland's most exclusive French restaurants. It had opened within the past year, to much fanfare, and reservations quickly became impossible to get. Eliot, however, had simply called a few hours before they arrived to reserve a table.

The chef at L'Epicure was well-known for his emphasis on taste and flavor. But most of the food was served in the form of small cubes—hardly enough for two hungry medical professionals coming off a busy shift.

Bria's duck confit with field greens was a small cube of—presumably—duck, about the size of half a domino, and two lettuce leaves, artfully placed so they crossed one another.

She poked again at the cube dubiously. "Is it supposed to bounce?"

"I think the bouncing is what makes it fancy," said Eliot. His own small cube of sea bass seemed even smaller in the center of the vast, otherwise empty white plate.

Their waiter approached to ask if they were ready for the next course.

"What is it?" Eliot asked.

"Lobster roe, bathed in a sea of crème fraîche."

Bria's heart sank. Why was the most expensive food always the most unappetizing? She was all too familiar with these kinds of restaurants, though it had been a long time since she'd set foot in one. The restaurant was so focused on being exclusive that it had forgotten to make sure to serve good food. In her experience, the quality of the food didn't matter in a place like this. No one ate it. People came to places like this to see who was here and to be seen themselves.

The waiter removed their plates and set the next course in front of them. Bria looked at Eliot with pleading eyes.

"What's wrong?" he said. "Don't you like your, um…your fish eggs?"

At that, they both burst out laughing.

"I'm not sure this type of place is my thing anymore," she said.

"It's kind of a bust, isn't it?" he replied. "I was hoping that coming here might be a nice change of pace for you, since I got the impression that it's been quite some time since you went anywhere really special for a meal."

She picked her fork up and then set it down decidedly. There was simply no way she could eat the dish in front of her. "I think I've been a midwife for too long for this to count as an actual dinner."

"Damn. Guess my timing was off."

She gave him a quizzical look, and he explained. "I wanted to impress you. Back when we were dating, I always wanted to take you to a fancy restaurant."

"But we went to nice places all the time."

"Yes, but you paid for our meals. You got the

reservations that were impossible to get. I, on the other hand, was lucky if I could dig enough money out of my sofa cushions to pay for pizza once in a while."

"Oh, Eliot, what does it matter who paid for anything? You were my fiancé. I never resented having to pay for things. I was always happy to share with you, to make both of our lives better."

"Yes, because you could afford it."

"So what? What difference does that make? You'd have done the same if our positions were reversed. In fact, this dinner proves it. Our positions *are* reversed. Am I supposed to feel embarrassed and insecure because you're taking me out to a dinner I can't afford myself?" An even worse thought occurred to her. "Or is this supposed to be some attempt to pay me back for all the times I took you out while you were dating? As though I was keeping some weird sort of ledger system regarding who spent what?"

"No! Not at all." He seemed to be struggling to explain, and she tried to be patient. She wanted to understand. "I did want to be able to take you somewhere nice tonight. Yes, because of the past. But not in the way you're describing. I only wanted you to enjoy yourself. I was hoping to impress you."

"But you do impress me. Your medical skills

impress me. Who you are as a person impresses me. I don't care about what restaurants you can get reservations at or what you can buy. That's not the kind of thing that matters to me."

"But it does matter to some people."

"I've already told you those people don't matter! Why does what other people think have to be important at all?"

His face had a familiar withdrawn expression. She wondered if he was going to shut down, just as he always had every time a conversation got emotional. Six years wasn't nearly enough time to make her forget that pattern: they'd disagree, he'd shut down and she'd feel abandoned and hurt. But this time, instead of withdrawing into himself and leaving her feeling alone and confused, he seemed to think better of it.

"Because sometimes those people will treat you differently. Look, I agree with what you're saying. The best way to deal with other people's judgment is to not care about it. But you have to understand that the cost of being yourself and not caring what other people think is different for me than it is for you."

She wanted to hear more. "Go on."

"I've been trying to live in two different worlds ever since I got into high school," he explained. Bria knew he'd attended an elite prep school in the city. "Word got around that I was a scholarship student, despite my best efforts to keep anyone from finding out. People started spreading rumors that I was poor. Which was true, but you know how cruel kids can be."

"Children can be absolutely horrible little monsters, and that's coming from a midwife who loves children."

"That may be the case, but ultimately children learn their views from their parents. Some of my friends at school had actual live-in servants in their houses. How do you think their parents treated those servants?

"I can't imagine."

"Well, I have a pretty good guess, because my mother started cleaning some of my classmates' houses after the hotel she worked at shut down. I was so embarrassed. I begged her not to tell anyone she was my mother. And the worst part was, she understood."

"Why was that the worst part?"

"Because there was no reason for either of us to be embarrassed. Cleaning houses is honest work for honest pay. When she agreed to keep it a secret, it was as though she was agreeing that we had something to be ashamed of."

"Eliot, you were only a child. You were just trying to fit in."

"I suppose…but at the time, I felt as though I was betraying our family by not wanting to tell anyone what my mother did. I went to great lengths to keep the secret. I'd try to come up with excuses to keep from having to invite my friends over to our one-bedroom apartment after school. I'd tell them that my mother was away on business, or that we were having our pool cleaned. But I'd go over to their houses. Until, of course, the inevitable happened."

"What was that?"

"One of my friends… I think his name was Langdon…he invited a group of kids over after school to play video games. I was so excited. It was the newest game system. And Langdon lived in this huge thirteen-bedroom mansion. I remember his housekeeper greeted us with snacks, and it was the most substantial meal I'd had all day. I didn't like bringing my lunches to school, you see, because my mother always packed me bologna sandwiches on white bread, and I was embarrassed for the other kids to see how sparse my lunches were. It would have just fueled the rumors that I was poor.

"Anyway, we went into the kitchen to get some more snacks, and there was my mother, cleaning."

"That must have been hard. You were with all of your friends, after all."

"But she was my mother." He paused, and Bria could see it was hard for him to tell this story. "At first, her face lit up when she saw me. But then one of my friends asked if we knew each other. And I said no.

"And I saw her expression slip into nonrecognition. She was going to cover for me. And I couldn't stand it. I said, 'Actually, she's my mother,' and I walked around their expensive kitchen island with the granite countertop and hugged her."

"Oh, she must have been so proud of you."

"Maybe. I can't forget the look on her face when she decided to cover for me. I swore I'd never deny her, or myself, ever again. But there were consequences. The biggest was that I became a total outcast at school. There were no more invitations to play video games with anyone after school. I got picked last for all the team sports."

"I want to repeat what I said before about children being little monsters."

He sighed. "And I'll repeat what I said about their parents."

She couldn't disagree with him.

"College and medical school were better, though," he continued. "Medical school was a great equalizer, because even though there were people from wealthy families, merit and skill counted for a lot. It didn't matter quite so much where you came from, as long as you performed well and got good grades. Or, at least, while in school it didn't matter. After graduation, the people you're connected to made a big difference in the kinds of jobs everyone landed. I saw lots of people beat out better candidates for jobs because they had relationships with major donors or people on the board of directors."

"Hmm, that's a problem we know about all too well," Bria said, rolling her eyes.

"Indeed we do. So I went into business, to give myself some more freedom, and so I could take care of my mother. She's retired to a mansion in Aruba now."

As she listened to Eliot's story, she realized that independence was just as important to him as it was to her. He'd needed to make money to gain his independence, just as she'd needed to give it up to gain hers.

"I'm sorry," she said heavily. "I should have been more perceptive to how you felt about money, especially because I grew up with my father and saw how he manipulated everyone with it. I learned from birth that money was his way of exerting control. I could have anything I wanted, as long as it was something that he wanted to buy me. So I could have the best of everything, but not necessarily what I wanted."

"I'm sure that was hard." She couldn't tell

if he was being serious or not, so she tried to explain.

"It was, actually." She tried to think of how to put it into words. "When I was six, an animal shelter had an adoption event downtown, and I begged my parents for a dog. I wanted the sweet brown mutt they had at the shelter. But my father refused to get anything other than a purebred Samoyed. That dog was incredibly bad-tempered and terrorized me for ten years. But my father didn't care, because it looked perfect in our family pictures. He had to control everything, and if I fought against it, it meant I was spoiled, because how could anyone fight against having their life handed to them on a silver platter? But everything I had was completely on his terms."

"So you gave it all up," he said. His voice seemed uneasy. She wondered if it was hard for him to hear her talking about stepping away from her family's fortune when he'd worked so hard for his.

"I needed to build something for myself. And I found midwifery, which allowed me to do that." She laughed. "It seems ironic now that you found your freedom in business, and I found mine in the medical field."

He hesitated and then said, "I don't know that I've found much enjoyment in the business world. But independence, yes. It's going to be hard to leave the hospital in a few weeks. The partners want me to give up my medical license for good so I can focus on the firm full-time, and the only way I could convince them to let me have these six weeks off was to promise that I would."

"You mentioned to me before you were thinking about giving it up, but seriously, why would you do that?"

"I think I have to. The partners are depending on me."

"Yes, to make them more money. But there are patients depending on you, too. It's a lot harder to find a good, compassionate doctor than someone who wants to make a million dollars. I think you could help a lot more people as a doctor than as a millionaire."

"I'd like to think so, but it's not that simple. If I'm not there to lead the firm, and it loses money, that affects the salaries and job security of many medical professionals. I've been in it for too long now, and at this point I don't see that there's any other way out."

She could see that it was a tough choice for him, but she had a feeling that his career in business hadn't left him feeling very happy. From what she'd seen at the hospital, working with patients made his face light up. He brought an energy to working out difficult diagnoses and helping patients overcome obstacles that she hadn't seen from other doctors. But the expression on his face when he discussed his business career simply looked...dull. As though he was talking about a tiresome chore or discouraging weather.

But at least he was talking about it now. That was a big difference from what she remembered from six years ago and even when he'd first mentioned it to her a couple of weeks ago. He'd never talked about anything. When something was bothering him, he'd always hidden it. She'd always wondered why.

"How come we never talked about these things while we were dating?" she asked him.

He shrugged. "What difference would it have made?"

She couldn't believe it. "Eliot, it would have made *all* the difference." Knowing what Eliot had gone through as a child made his insecurity around money make so much more sense to her now. "Didn't you think I'd understand?"

"The trouble was that *I* didn't understand. It wasn't until long after medical school that I realized I'd tried to fit into two worlds for so long that I'd forgotten how to be myself. When I was younger, and when I was with you, I dealt with things by trying to be the person I thought people wanted to see. But then, with my family, or even in medical school, I didn't want anyone to know how much I was pretending not to be myself. So I hid that, too. The result was that I couldn't be myself anywhere. It felt as though I'd almost forgotten how. And when we broke up, I knew I couldn't try to get back together with you, because as long as we were together, I'd still be trying to fit into your world instead of figuring myself out."

She couldn't help saying, "I thought we could figure ourselves out together."

"No, we couldn't. I was always going to be Bria Thomas's plus-one, instead of my own person."

"But you never even tried to explain this to me. You just held it all in. You're doing the same thing with medicine right now. You're just assuming it can't happen. Maybe if you'd actually talk about this dilemma, you might understand more how you feel about it. I've seen you with patients—and I've seen how they respond to you. You don't belong in a boardroom. You belong in a hospital. I understand why money is important to you, but really, how much more do you need? It doesn't seem to have made you any more secure in yourself."

She instantly regretted her words, worried that she'd spoken out of heat and gone too far.

"I don't belong in a boardroom, do I? Well, thank you very much for telling me. Maybe you can do what you do best and make all of my decisions without asking me."

"I'd love to ask you, Eliot, I'd love to know how you feel, but I need to know that you'll actually tell me instead of shutting down."

"Maybe it's hard to tell someone how I feel when they've already decided what's best for me. It's easy to ask how much money I need when you've had everything you need for your entire life."

"But I gave all that up, Eliot."

"It was still your choice to do that. You could have done a lot of good with that money. For all you know, if you hadn't given up your fortune, you wouldn't need to scramble to raise money for the center now."

"That's not how it works and you know it. My father controls the family trust. Any money from him would have come with major strings attached. And I don't see how you get to judge my financial decisions. Or any of my life decisions, really."

"The way you were just judging mine, you mean?"

"I wasn't trying to judge. I was trying to understand how you feel!"

"Well, maybe you can't."

She put her head in her hands, exasperated. It was so frustrating that they always seemed to arrive back at the same place, no matter how hard they tried not to.

"I'm sorry," Eliot said suddenly. He reached across the table and took her hand.

"What?" She blinked. "Why are you apologizing? I'm the one who spoke out of line first."

"But I'm the one who said we should keep things physical. No trying to rehash the past, no relationship stuff. And yet here we are."

He was right. They'd agreed not to talk about the past, and yet somehow it had a way of coming into the present. And every time it did, they found themselves having a different version of the same old fight.

"We need a reset button," she said.

"Want to start over?" he asked.

"Only if we can start over at a place with some better food."

He poked again at the unappetizing glob on his plate. "This place has two Michelin stars. I'm not sure if there's a better place in Portland."

She smiled and rose from her chair. "I can think of one."

Half an hour later, Bria's eyes closed in pleasure as she sank her teeth into the cheeseburger from the greasy spoon around the corner from the hospital.

"Of all the places we could eat, this is what you wanted," said Eliot, cautiously inspecting his chili.

"Mmm… Now this is a meal. This is real food, not tiny little experiments on plates."

"If I'd known all those years ago that a cheeseburger could smooth things over so easily, we both might have been a lot happier."

She crumpled a napkin and threw it across the table at him playfully. "Hush. Just enjoy the moment." She took another bite. "This diner is the restaurant that should be charging exorbitant prices, not that fancy place up the street. This right here is the breakfast of champions."

"But we're not having breakfast."

"You're right. Maybe we should pick up some extra in case we need to refuel tomorrow morning."

"For breakfast? That sounds unappealing in about eight different ways."

"I know, but hear me out. Babies come at all different times, with absolutely no regard for conventional mealtimes. As a midwife, you get used to eating what you need when you can, rather than worrying about whether your food is appropriate for whatever mealtime it's supposed to be."

"Rather like traveling to different time zones and craving pizza when you arrive somewhere at nine in the morning."

"Exactly." She ate a French fry with great satisfaction. "I can't believe we didn't come here first. I'll take one of these burgers over haute cuisine any time of day."

"Hmm. Well, you *could* take away some cold diner food for breakfast. Or you could try what I think would be a far more enjoyable option."

"And what might that be?"

"Something you don't know about me is that over the past six years, I've nearly perfected the Spanish omelet."

She smiled. "Are you offering to make me breakfast in the morning?"

"Not just any breakfast. I'm offering to make you the best breakfast you've ever had."

She didn't doubt it.

CHAPTER SEVEN

BRIA STARED AT the unopened box, wondering what to do.

The past few weeks had been a blur of work, preparation for the charity gala and nights with Eliot. She'd never been so busy in her life.

She'd been worried that her purely physical fling with Eliot would complicate her life. But as she'd spent long days planning, organizing and generating publicity for the gala, she'd found it all much easier now that she no longer had to spend so much time trying not to think about him. Now that they'd given in to their physical attraction, she didn't have to worry if he noticed a sidelong glance. She didn't have to question whether a look he gave her meant that he was attracted to her. She knew the answer. He *wanted* her. And knowing that he wanted her meant that she didn't have to put so much energy into hiding how much she wanted him.

He would be gone in two weeks. Despite their

agreement to keep things on a purely physical level, she knew that when he left, she would be sad. But she also knew that she needed to accept her time with Eliot for what it was: a second chance to end their relationship on peaceful terms. She couldn't allow herself to want anything more than that. And as long as she didn't, she wouldn't have to worry about getting hurt.

Experience had shown that getting emotionally involved with Eliot was a mistake for both of them. Every time they discussed the past, and every time they tried to discuss their feelings for one another, they ended up fighting. Somehow, when she was with him, she couldn't seem to find the right words to express how she felt. And she knew all too well how difficult that was for him. She felt their choice not to allow things to go beyond the physical had been the right one for them both.

But she found it hard to keep herself from getting emotionally involved when Eliot did things that were so unexpected.

Like the box, for example.

It was a pale blue box with a large silver ribbon around it. It had been delivered to her door that morning, but she hadn't had time to open it. A lifetime ago, she'd had such boxes delivered to her home by the dozens. But she hadn't seen one in years.

There was a note from Eliot underneath the ribbon.

Just in case you still need something to wear.

The truth was, she did need something. She'd been so busy that she hadn't had time to rent a ball gown until the last minute, and the one she'd nabbed wasn't exactly flattering on her petite frame. It was formalwear, and it was within her price range, so it would have to do. Hazel had offered to lend her something, but Bria was far too short, and her sewing skills weren't even close to good enough for her to hem up six inches of one of Hazel's dresses.

She didn't want to wear the rented dress, but it wasn't as though she had a range of other options. As the coordinator of the gala, she needed something formal. All eyes would be on her, and she'd be representing the center. The rented dress might not be the best thing she'd ever worn, but at least it was serviceable, and she'd resigned herself to wearing it.

But then the box had arrived. If she was surprised to see it, she was even more surprised to see that it was from Eliot.

She'd held back from opening it for a moment, uncertain of what the box might mean.

They'd agreed that their relationship was purely physical. No emotions, no attachment.

So what could he possibly be thinking by sending her a couture dress?

She opened the box with tentative fingers and couldn't help emitting a small gasp when she saw the gown. It was a dark green, the same color as her eyes, made of sleek satin. It was strapless, with a sweetheart neckline and a fluted skirt with a hem that rose up in front just a bit, enough to show off a pair of high heels, and then came down behind her to brush the floor in the barest hint of a train. It had been years since she'd worn anything so beautiful.

And—wonder of wonders—it had pockets.

Gorgeous and functional. The perfect dress for the midwife who needed to slip back into princess mode, just for one night.

Since Bria had become a midwife, her life had gotten considerably less glamorous than it used to be. She spent her days dealing with squirmy newborns, placentas and all the delightful bodily fluids that were involved in the natural order of childbirth.

But that didn't mean she'd forgotten her knowledge of high fashion. This gown had easily cost several thousand dollars, and quite possibly more. It was an incredibly generous gift. He'd remembered their conversation about how she'd sold all her fashionable dresses. She was touched.

Then again, Eliot had made it sound as though a few thousand dollars was the kind of money he might find lying within his couch cushions now.

Still, he couldn't have known how much a dress like this, on a night like this, would mean to her. She'd been to plenty of galas in the past, but this was her event, for her cause, and it was also a celebration of every way she'd changed and everything she'd built over the past six years.

She hesitated, wondering if she could even wear the dress. If Eliot's gift meant far more to her than it did to him, then by wearing it, would she be crossing the boundaries they'd set for their arrangement?

They'd said no emotions. But she didn't think she could wear this dress without getting emotional.

She decided to call Hazel for advice.

"Damn," Hazel said once Bria tried the dress on in front of her. "He even knows your size. Are you *sure* you understand the terms of the arrangement you two have? Because this dress is not the kind of thing you get for the ex you're just having a short-term affair with."

Bria shook her head. "I don't know. We both agreed that we were keeping things strictly physical, but this…this is too much. I can't accept a gift like this, can I?"

Hazel was still rummaging through the box the dress had come in. "Oh, my. Did you see that it comes with gloves as well? You are going to look absolutely gorgeous."

"But I can't wear it, Hazel. We agreed that this was just sex. And now he's sending me one of the nicest dresses I've ever seen, to wear to the most important gala I've ever attended." With the most significant man from her past in attendance, she thought, but didn't say. "This dress has to mean something, doesn't it? He couldn't just have sent it to me on a whim."

Hazel pursed her lips. "What do you think it means?"

"I have no idea. All this time, I thought that getting back together was just a way for us to say goodbye. But now there's this dress. I thought we'd agreed we just wanted closure. Was I wrong? Does he want more? Is he going to think *I* want more if I wear this?"

"Let's step back about twenty paces. Maybe you're overthinking this. You said he's rich now, right? Maybe the dress isn't some grand, romantic gesture. Maybe he just knew that you were rushing to get everything done, up to the last minute, and he wanted to do something nice for you."

It was possible. Maybe he didn't think of the dress as a terribly expensive gift but simply as a kind gesture.

Though the neckline of the dress was awfully low for a kind gesture.

"What do you think I should do, Hazel?"

"Well, it's strapless, so I definitely recommend some long earrings. And with the way the hem rises in the front, you'll need a killer pair of heels to show off. I can let you borrow mine. I've got some Hermès stilettos my grandmother gave me for Christmas."

"Hazel! I mean what do I do about the fact that the dress is from Eliot?"

"Does something need to be done about it?"

"Of course it does! If I wear it, what kind of message does that send?"

Hazel eyed the dress's swooping neckline. "A strong one."

Bria pleaded with Hazel to be serious.

"I'm trying to be," Hazel replied. "Look, the two of you are just together for now, right? He's going back to Boston in a couple of weeks, and then, presumably, he'll be out of your life for good."

"That's the plan," Bria said weakly.

"So as your best friend, while I don't think this fling is the *wisest* plan you've ever come up with, I can kind of see the appeal. But if he's going to be gone in two weeks, what are you afraid of? Don't hold back. Put the rental back in the closet. Wear the hot dress. Be spectacular tonight. Give him something to remember two weeks from now."

Bria tilted her chin, bolstered by her friend's words. Hazel was right. No matter what, Eliot would be gone in two weeks. Nothing would change just because she was getting emotional over a dress. She might as well wear it and enjoy herself.

And if the thought of Eliot leaving made her heart crack just a bit, she'd just have to let herself worry about that when it happened. After he was gone, she could let herself become emotional. But if she wanted him for now, she'd have to keep her feelings to herself. They'd said no emotions, and she planned to stick to that agreement. Otherwise, she'd end up spoiling her one chance at finding closure over their relationship.

This time, when Eliot left, she didn't want to feel devastated. Instead, she wanted them both to feel as though they could move on. And she wouldn't accomplish that if she indulged in daydreams about a future that would never be. Even if part of her wanted the dress to be more than just a thoughtful gesture, she needed to accept that it wasn't. Because in two weeks, Eliot would be gone, and she wanted to be mentally prepared for that. And so, instead of wishing for anything more, she should focus on tonight and give both of them something to remember after he left.

Eliot pulled up to the entrance of the event hall in his Lamborghini and handed his keys to the valet. Dusk was just beginning to fall. He was a little early, but he didn't mind. He hoped Bria would wear the dress he'd sent her, and if she did, he didn't want to miss her entrance.

He couldn't explain what had possessed him to buy her a dress. But as he'd watched her prepare for the gala over the last few weeks and seen how important its success was to her, he'd wanted to help in any way he could. He could make a donation, of course, but he wanted to do something more personal. At the last minute, he'd remembered their conversation about clothes and decided to send her something she might like. And even though they'd agreed not to become romantically involved, he didn't think it was too far out of the bounds of their arrangement for him to get her a dress. Tonight was important to her, and she'd needed something to wear other than the rental gown he'd spotted in her closet.

He had to admit, too, that it felt good to be able to do something to help her, for once. When they'd been together, she'd always bought things for him: clothes for practicum interviews, tickets to events. He'd tried to accept those things graciously, but he couldn't help resenting that their relationship seemed so imbalanced. It was nice to finally be able to return the favor and offer her something that she needed. It helped provide the sense of closure he was looking for.

The event hall was a Tudor-style mansion, with a long stone pathway leading to heavy wood doors. Glittering partygoers walked under a tunnel of archways covered with ivy and softly glowing fairy lights. With only a few weeks to plan, Bria had made the event look like something on a par with a major awards ceremony. Given how much money the center needed to raise, she'd known she would need an event that would attract the kind of people who didn't just want to donate money but wanted to make the news while doing so. Judging by the amount of opulence around him, she might have pulled it off.

In the past, these kinds of events had always bored him to tears. But tonight's atmosphere seemed more relaxed. The gala was somehow glamorous without feeling formal. Maybe it was because he knew so many people. Most of the staff from St. Raymond's were there. Dr. Anderson, the hospital's chief of staff, gave him a wave before taking over the dance floor with an enthusiastic jitterbug. Caleb and Hazel arrived and immediately engaged Eliot in conversation. Hazel gave him a few knowing looks that confirmed his assumption that Bria had indeed told her everything. He'd also invited a few of his friends from Boston, because he thought they might be willing to donate to Bria's cause, and he was pleasantly surprised when they showed up.

He had to admit that he was actually having fun.

There were even a few patients who'd come to support the Women's Health Center. Sandra Patterson, the soon-to-be mother of quints, was there, her husband spinning her around in her wheelchair. She'd made it to thirty-three weeks of pregnancy despite her frustration with constant bed rest. Her cervical stitch, which had been put in earlier on in her pregnancy to prevent her from miscarrying, had already been taken out in preparation for the labor, so she was good to go as soon as her babies gave her the green light. It couldn't be much longer now, so he'd given her medical clearance to attend the gala tonight under strict conditions. Mental stimulation was so important to women restricted to bed rest, and she'd been growing so despondent that he'd thought the outing would do her more good than harm. She looked happier than she'd been in weeks.

As the song ended, he crossed the dance floor to speak to Sandra.

"Not too much excitement, remember. And you're expected to leave within the hour."

Sandra rolled her eyes. "I know, Doctor. Home by 9:00 p.m., or I'll turn into a pumpkin."

"And don't you forget it."

Someone came up behind him and took his hand. "You're off duty tonight, Doctor. Let's allow Sandra to enjoy her evening out."

He turned around to see Bria. She was wearing the dress he'd sent her. The low, strapless neckline clung to her perfectly. She'd worn the silk gloves as well; her hand, which still held his, felt light and smooth as water. She was gorgeous. The dress was made even more beautiful by the fact that she was wearing it.

He tried to greet her, but his voice caught in his throat. She looked positively delectable. Seeing her like this was having more of an effect on him than he'd anticipated.

For the first time, he found himself thinking about his departure in two weeks with a pang of regret. It would be hard to say goodbye to her again. But also necessary, for both their sakes. He needed to move on. And he was sure he would, eventually. But not right now. Not tonight. Tonight, he wanted to enjoy the vision of Bria in the fairy-tale gown he'd bought her. And to fantasize about taking the gown off her later, if the opportunity arose.

The band struck up again, and he found his voice at last. He lifted her hand to his lips. "I wonder if we could dance?"

She smiled. "That's what we're here for. That, and to raise a whole lot of money."

He took her hand and put an arm around her waist. He'd planned to make a large donation himself, and he was about to tell Bria about it, but then he stopped himself. Bria had worked hard on the gala. He didn't want to flaunt his wealth by bragging about how much he could donate. Better to do it quietly, he decided, and keep the donation anonymous.

When he and Bria were together, there had been so many times when he'd felt as though they were on uneven footing. But over the past few years, he'd built his career and grown more secure in himself. And now that the tables were turned and he was the one able to help Bria, he had a perspective on their relationship that was different than the one he'd held for the past few years. Her family's wealth might have made him uncomfortable, but it was never Bria herself who'd tried to make him feel that way. He'd been uncomfortable because of the situation, not because of her. He'd had a chip on his shoulder about money for years, yet Bria hadn't put it there. It was there because of the bullies he'd gone to private school with and the medical students from wealthy families who'd looked down on him. Students who hadn't really wanted to be doctors but were there because it was the only career their families thought was respectable enough.

Calvin Thomas had probably been one of those medical students once, he realized. Coming from such a wealthy family, he couldn't just have any career. No, he'd have to be a surgeon, an eminent one, because nothing else would satisfy the family's pride. He doubted Calvin had chosen his career out of a desire to help people. Everything the man did was about how things would look to someone else.

Bria laid her head against his shoulder as they swayed about the floor. She was so unlike the rest of her family. And with that thought, his certainty grew: something—or should he say, some*one*—had influenced her to break up with him that night six years ago. She'd always insisted it was her own choice, but he had his suspicions that Calvin had played a part in it. At the time, he'd given in to his own fears instead of thinking it through logically. He hadn't believed she was really so materialistic, but his own fear that he wasn't good enough had erased his doubt and led him to accept her words at face value.

But now Bria's life looked nothing like what he would have expected of someone who was selfish, materialistic and spoiled. Because she *wasn't* those things. Since he'd earned his millions, he'd met plenty of women who were only interested in money. None of them were anything like Bria. None of them had passion for their careers, or worked with service organizations, or with patients whom they genuinely cared for. Bria was different. She wasn't the kind of person who cared about background or financial status.

He should have known that about her back then as well. But he'd been too afraid to believe it. Too insecure, too defensive. There was still too much of the young boy in him who'd been bullied so harshly about who he was and where he came from. But he wasn't that boy anymore. He was secure in himself now, and he had a right to know the truth.

He and Bria might have agreed not to discuss the past, but he needed answers. If they were going to find the closure they were looking for, he wanted to know the real reason she'd broken up with him. He didn't buy that it had been her choice. Not for a moment. And he wondered how on earth he'd ever been convinced that it had.

He held her body closer against his, marveling at how perfectly they fit together as they danced. He was so glad she didn't wear perfume. For as long as he'd known her, she'd smelled like coffee, and vanilla, and herself, and he couldn't imagine any combination of scents that he preferred more.

He'd lost count of how many events like this they'd attended when they were together. He'd always felt obligated to go, and he'd never enjoyed himself. This time, he was almost disappointed when the band ended their song and began something faster. Bria's eyes lit up, and he could tell she wanted to keep dancing, but suddenly her smile faded.

"What's wrong?"

Her expression hardened. "Don't turn around, but my father's here."

Eliot's jaw tightened. "Perfect. I'd like to go talk to him."

"Wait! Please don't. I mean, don't bother. He isn't worth getting upset over."

Eliot disagreed, but he saw the panic in Bria's eyes and decided not to pursue the point. He had plenty to say to Calvin Thomas, but he didn't want Bria's event to be spoiled by a confrontation.

"I didn't know you'd decided to invite him."

"I didn't. But I should have known he'd show up anyway. This is a major charity event. *Of course* all his friends would expect him to be here. And everyone would talk if he didn't attend a gala hosted by his own daughter. He couldn't stay away."

Eliot could see the rage burning in her eyes. A minute ago, he'd been worried about causing a scene and spoiling Bria's gala; now he had a feeling she might be on her way to accomplishing that herself. "Do you want me to see about having security remove him from the building? They might be able to do it quietly." And judging by the look in her eyes, they might prevent her from tearing off Calvin's head.

"No need," she said, her lips forming a firm line. "Stay here for just a minute. I'm going to go deal with him myself." She stalked off the dance floor, her face so furious that Eliot could almost pity Calvin. Almost.

Bria elbowed her way through the crowd of gala attendees, trying to fix a smile on her face as she nodded to each patron who waved at her. Inside, she was seething. Her father had absolutely no right to be here. Six years ago, he'd ruined the most important thing in her life when he'd threatened Eliot. She refused to allow him to cast a shadow over her career as well.

In a way, she was glad he was here. The past few weeks with Eliot had shown her exactly what she'd given up—their physical connection, the way they worked together so seamlessly, the way he seemed to anticipate her needs. She'd walked away from it all once, because her father had been in control. But he couldn't control her any longer. She knew it, and it was time for him to know it, too. Elliot had enough of his own money and prestige now and couldn't be threatened by him anymore, and she had earned her own independence. For the first time in her life, she was ready to tell her father that he couldn't bully her ever again.

She reached the edge of the crowd, where her father stood. His face was grim, his brow furrowed, but she could match him glower for glower, and she wasn't afraid to let him know it.

"Hello, Dad. What brings you here?"

He scowled at her. "Don't be ridiculous. A few weeks ago I learned that you were putting on a major event at extremely short notice, despite knowing that doing so would throw you into the public eye and subject you to all the scrutiny that is typical for a member of the Thomas family."

"Well, I managed to pull it all together, and

disaster didn't strike. Despite what you may believe about me, I was actually able to accomplish something on my own. The world hasn't
ended, and as you can see, the gala is going
very smoothly."

"I disagree. For one thing, my invitation seems
to have been lost in the mail."

"It wasn't lost. You weren't invited."

"You call that good event planning? How do
you think it will look when it's reported in the
press that you didn't invite your own father to
your fund-raising gala? What kind of publicity
would that create for your little charity? I saved
you by coming here tonight."

She bristled. "The center is doing just fine
on its own. It doesn't need saving, especially
by you."

"No? Then I suppose you just got everyone
out here in their finest getup for fun, then."

The anger, already strong within her, threatened to overflow. There was nothing she hated
more than when her father was right, and he
was right on both counts: she *had* been worried
about how it would look to other potential donors if she didn't invite her father, and the center
was in a financial crisis. But she hadn't worked
this hard over the past few weeks to allow her
father to swoop in and act as though he'd res-
cued her from the brink of disaster.

He pulled out his checkbook. "I may as well do my part, since it seems you're so committed to your little scheme. How much do you need?"

She scowled. "No, Dad. Your money isn't welcome here."

"Oh, really? I wonder how your friend Hazel might feel if she heard you say that."

"Your money always comes with strings attached."

"That's how the world works. It's best you learn now that everyone owes somebody something."

"Even where family is concerned? Even where love is involved?"

"The sooner you give up all of your idealistic fantasies, the better off you'll be."

"If those are fantasies, I'm going to do my best to make them a reality," she retorted.

"There you go again, showing your typically bad judgment. Making all your typical bad decisions," he jeered.

"Every decision I've made since I stepped back from the family has brought me to exactly where I wanted to be."

"Really? Living in that tiny apartment? Working as a *nurse*?"

"I'm a nurse-midwife, actually. And I don't have to care about your opinions anymore. Neither does Eliot. You can't threaten his career again. He's been very successful on his own, no thanks to you. You can't control either one of us."

"Ha! He's been successful on his own, has he? No thanks to me? Is that what he's let you think? That he's one of those idealistic types? Don't be so naive. There are some things about him that I know better than you, my girl."

"You don't know him at all."

"Oh, but I do. You think he made all those millions of his on his own? Nonsense. Everybody in this room owes me something, including him. You don't believe me? Ask him. He'll tell you. He thinks he's honorable, after all."

Bria had no idea what he was talking about, but she was so angry that she didn't want to hear another word.

"Dad, if you want to stay, you're welcome to do so. If you want to donate money, fine. But know that I can do this without you. In fact, that's what I need most from you tonight. Not your money, but your confidence that I can do something on my own. And I can do it all far better without you involved."

She stormed out of the ballroom, leaving him sputtering over his drink at the edge of the crowd.

She scanned the hallway for a private corner where she could compose herself and opted for the stairwell, next to the elevators. She leaned against the wall and took a few deep breaths.

She should have known her father would show up uninvited. He claimed to care so much about appearances, but it was just like him not to care about anyone else's feelings. He wasn't the kind of person who worried about whether he was welcome or not. He simply showed up, caused his havoc and then left everyone else to deal with the consequences. It was a pattern that had repeated itself constantly throughout her childhood.

It was therefore no small pleasure to be able to tell him exactly what she thought, and to leave him choking on his drink. She smiled. No matter what else happened this evening, telling her father off had been deeply satisfying.

Now that she was feeling more composed, she realized she should get back to the ballroom to see what Eliot was up to.

But just as she turned to leave the stairwell, she encountered Sandra Patterson, her husband pushing her wheelchair.

"Heading home for the night?" Bria pushed the button for the elevator for them.

"I'm afraid so," said Sandra. "Those are the doctor's orders. It was wonderful to be out for an evening, even if it was only for an hour."

"I'll see you down to the first floor."

"We don't want to trouble you," said Sandra.

"It's no trouble at all." Bria stepped on the elevator after the Pattersons.

The elevator seemed to be taking a strangely long time to travel only one floor. Bria and the Pattersons waited and then exchanged confused glances. A moment later, the elevator began moving, and they all relaxed.

"There it goes," Dan Patterson said, relieved.

But then the elevator came to an abrupt stop, and the doors didn't open.

"What's the matter?" said Sandra, her voice worried.

"I'll check." Bria hit the button to open the doors. Nothing. Then the elevator moved a bit lower before coming to a sudden stop. The doors opened…to reveal an inch of space between the bottom of the doors and the next floor.

"Oh, dear," Bria said. "It looks like we're stuck." She pressed the emergency service button, which blinked on and off but gave no other indication of what might happen next. "Not to worry. I've got my phone with me. We can call for help, and hopefully we'll get out of here before too long."

Sandra winced. "I hope so. These babies seem to think they're trying out for a world gymnastics team. I've been getting so many little pokes and kicks today."

Bria examined Sandra's face more closely. "Have the babies been more active than usual?"

"All day long. I think they're all doing somersaults in there. But a few minutes ago, they really started kicking."

"Why didn't you say anything?" Dan asked.

"I didn't think it was any different than usual. Between the five of them, someone's always giving me a good kick. But it usually stops much sooner than this. And—ouch! They usually don't kick quite so hard."

Bria put her hand on Sandra's stomach and felt her own body grow cold with dread. "Sandra, those aren't kicks. You're having contractions."

CHAPTER EIGHT

BRIA TRIED TO calm the panic rising within her. This couldn't be happening. Not here.

Dan Patterson seemed to be thinking along the same lines. "What do you mean, she's having contractions?"

"Exactly what I said."

"But the elevator's stuck! She can't have the babies now. It's the worst possible moment."

"I agree with you, Dan, but it's happening now, stuck elevator or not. But don't worry. Getting scared isn't going to help anything, and also, it's unnecessary, because we're going to do everything we can to get these babies delivered safely. We'll call an emergency services team that will get us out of here before you know it, and in the meantime, I'll be with you, Sandra and the babies every step of the way." She took her pager from her pocket and shot off the message—QUINTS911. She was about to put the pager away but then thought better of it and sent a second message: IN ELEVATOR.

Dan and Sandra looked terrified. "Dan," Bria said, trying to keep her voice even, "Sandra needs your help now. Can you take her hand and practice breathing, just like we've done in the practice sessions?"

Dan nodded and put his arm around Sandra's shoulders. Bria's cell phone rang—it was Eliot.

"Just got your page. Please tell me it doesn't mean what I think it means."

"Yep. The quints are on their way. Dan, Sandra and I are in the elevator near the south stairwell, stuck between the first and second floors."

"Any chance Sandra can make it to the hospital?"

Bria glanced at Sandra. "Maybe. Her water's broken, so it depends on how quickly you can get us out of here."

"Understood. We've already started making phone calls. Most of the quint team is here at the gala, so once we get you out of there, you'll have lots of support available. In the meantime, what do you need right now?"

Aside from nitroglycerin, for the heart attack she was about to have? Bria tried to keep her composure for the benefit of the Pattersons. "I need Hazel. Ask her to scrounge up any tools she can find for emergency premature birth.

Tell her there's an opening of about one inch between the elevator doors where someone could pass through small items."

"I'm on my way, along with the entire team. You're not alone. We'll all be right outside. And, Bria? You've got this."

She hung up, trying to take heart from his confident tone.

She turned to Sandra, who looked close to tears.

"I'm not going to have the babies in an elevator, am I?" asked Sandra. "Not after all those drills we practiced."

Bria made her voice as soothing as possible. "I know this isn't what you expected. But help is on the way, and they may have us out of here soon. And if not, I want you to know that I've delivered babies in stranger places than this." It was true. At least an elevator gave them four walls, a roof and overhead lighting. When she'd done her service work in Haiti, there'd been times she hadn't even had that.

She'd never had to deal with five babies at once, but she decided not to dwell on that detail right now.

She tried to prepare Sandra as best she could. "I want to get you out of that wheelchair. Just as a precaution. It'll be easiest to move you to the floor now rather than later." Bria and

Dan helped Sandra move to the floor, and Bria showed them how Sandra could be more comfortable if she positioned herself so she was leaning back against Dan.

"We need to do everything we can to slow your labor, so I want the two of you to continue to practice rhythmic breathing while I take a look at your cervix," she said.

Bria knelt to check on Sandra's progress, the skirt of her evening gown crumpling beneath her knees. So much for couture fashion. The ballroom floor seemed a million miles away. She'd have given anything to have Eliot here with her now.

Sandra was already five centimeters dilated. Unless something changed quickly, these babies were going to have quite a birthday story to tell. Assuming everything went smoothly. She tried not to think about the numerous things that could go wrong. As she'd told Dan earlier, fear wasn't going to help anything.

She heard a commotion outside the elevator doors, along with a great deal of banging. Did that mean rescuers were on their way? She didn't have time to give the question more than a fleeting thought, as she was giving all her attention to taking Sandra's pulse and helping her with her breathing. She was so absorbed in assessing Sandra's progress that Dan had to get her attention.

"Nurse Thomas? They're calling to you from outside."

"Oh!" She looked over to the gap in the doors, where Eliot and a firefighter had been trying to get her attention.

"The whole team's outside," said Eliot. "An ambulance has already arrived to whisk you off to the hospital the second the fire department can get you out. You and I can ride with Sandra, and the quint team will follow in their cars."

"That's a great plan, Eliot, but I'm not sure it does much to change our situation right now."

"This might. It's everything Hazel could get together." Eliot shoved a packet through the small opening.

Bria almost cried with relief. Hazel had included five gallon-size plastic bags—she must have found them in the event hall's kitchen—along with a shoelace, a single tea towel and a pair of scissors.

"We've got more tea towels if you need them. The hope is that we can get you out before it comes to that."

"The sooner, the better." Bria turned her attention back to Sandra, who was crying out as a strong contraction overtook her.

Bria took another look at Sandra's progress.

"Sandra, the first baby's coming very fast. I want you to keep breathing, just as you are now, but when the next contraction comes, I want you to push."

Sandra's eyes were wide with alarm. "But I thought you said we were going to try to slow down the labor!"

"I don't think we have any choice in the matter at this point. But look at me." She clasped Sandra's hand and held her gaze. "I'm going to do everything I can to give your babies the best start in life. You and Dan have protected them so well, and now we're all going to work together to make sure they arrive safely. That was always the plan. The way we follow that plan is just going to look a little different than we thought."

Sandra nodded, and when the next contraction came, she pushed and cried out.

"That's it, Sandra." Bria was relieved to see that the birth was proceeding fairly smoothly. If she hadn't known to expect multiple newborns, she would have felt that the birth was completely routine.

Routine was good. She had enough unexpected surprises to deal with at the moment; she didn't think she could handle any more.

Sandra's first child, a boy, made his way into the world and immediately demonstrated a healthy set of lungs. Bria laid him on the tea towel and used the shoelace from Hazel to clamp the cord. After a few minutes, during which she took the baby's vital signs as best she could, Bria cut the cord and then wrapped the baby in the tea towel and handed him to Sandra.

Sandra's face was aglow. "He's perfect."

Bria cut a hole for the baby's head in one of the large Ziploc bags. "You can hold him for a minute, but then I'll need to put one of these around him."

"A Ziploc bag?"

"I know it seems odd, but it's similar to what we'd use in the NICU to keep preemies warm. Here, I'll show you." Sandra handed her the baby. Keeping him wrapped in the tea towel, Bria deftly slipped his head through the hole so that the bag draped around his shoulders, like a poncho. She then sealed the edge of the bag and gave him back to Sandra.

"It's like a little rain suit," said Sandra.

At that moment, the elevator lurched and then proceeded smoothly to settle at the first floor. The doors opened, and Sandra was promptly surrounded by medical staff. They had her loaded into an ambulance in short order. Bria marveled at what seemed now like a surplus of medical equipment.

Within moments, Sandra had been loaded

into an ambulance. Eliot and Bria climbed in with her.

"City employees have temporarily closed some of the roads between here and the hospital," Eliot said. "We'll be there in no time at all."

By the time Sandra's second baby was born, they were already in the delivery room that had been set up during Eliot's drills. The last three babies were born by cesarean, which was far safer for the quintuplets, and easier on Sandra. The baby assembly line worked just as Eliot had planned, and since the hospital had set up five of every necessary piece of equipment ahead of time, everything was ready and waiting for the quints. Despite the chaotic way things had started, the rest of Sandra's labor couldn't have gone more smoothly.

As soon as the team ensured that all members of the now greatly extended Patterson family were resting comfortably, they left the delivery room to congratulate one another.

"Three babies in three minutes," Bria said to Eliot. "You would have broken that record if only things had gone according to plan."

He sighed. "The important thing is that all the babies are doing well. Maybe I'll have another chance to deliver quintuplets someday."

"Not if you quit medicine."

"Who knows? Hospitals aren't the only place

mothers give birth. There are all kinds of places that people need medical professionals. Elevators, for example." His eyes twinkled as he teased her. Then he grew more serious. "You did very well under incredible pressure."

Bria shook her head. "I tried not to show it, but I was so scared. I can't believe Sandra and the quints are all right."

"I can. They were in very good hands the entire time. You probably saved their lives."

"What saved their lives was having a well-trained team set up and ready to receive them at a moment's notice, which was your plan all along."

"Let's agree to call it a team effort, then."

She gave a weary smile as she stripped off the disposable surgical gown she'd put on over her eveningwear. No one had had time to put on regular gowns. Eliot checked the time. "What now?" he said. "There's still time to attend the last half hour of the gala. Do you want to head back and see how it's going?"

She was bone tired. "Let me check in with Hazel first. I'd rather not go back, to be honest. I'm exhausted, and I don't know if I can go back there without thinking about how I almost delivered five babies in an elevator."

Just as she fished her phone from her pocket,

she got a text from Hazel. "Oh my god! It looks like I don't have to go back after all!"

"Is something wrong?"

"Far from it. Hazel says we got an anonymous donation of two hundred and fifty thousand dollars right before the quints were born and that it pushed us well over our target amount." She flipped her phone case shut, her eyes sparkling.

"This has been quite a night for you," said Eliot. He had also taken off his disposable gown. He was still in his tuxedo, though he'd removed his black tie and loosened the top button of his collar. His jacket outlined his lean frame and the sharp angles of his shoulders.

She smiled back at him, flushed with success. But only for a moment. Her time with Eliot was growing so short.

But it was all she had, and so she might as well make the most of it.

"They can't need me at the gala now that we've exceeded our goal," she said. "I suppose I have the rest of the evening free."

"In that case, I know a great diner next door where you could show that dress off. Are you hungry? Neither of us got to eat at the gala."

"Starving."

"Care to accompany me to the finest of greasy spoons?"

"Only if we order it to go."

* * *

As hungry as they were, they didn't quite make it to dinner.

They'd brought cheeseburgers from the diner back to Bria's apartment. But when they entered, he dropped the bag on the kitchen counter and simply looked at her.

And the way he was looking made it seem as though he was starving, but not for food. He looked as though he wanted to devour *her*. He kept staring, eating her up with his eyes, and she kept letting him stare.

Tonight, she wasn't going to waste her last chance by thinking about how their fling couldn't last forever. Nothing lasted forever. That was life. For now, she just wanted to focus on what was in front of her.

Which, at the moment, was Eliot. Dressed in a tuxedo that outlined every firm line of his body.

He moved toward her, putting his hands around her waist. He bent to her ear and murmured, "I've been wanting to take this dress off you all night."

"And here I thought you wanted me to wear it."

"I'm glad you did. It definitely serves a purpose." He gave her a wicked smile.

"And what purpose is that, exactly?"

He placed his hands on her shoulders, and it was all she could do not to melt under his touch. His hands were cool, but her skin felt hot. She didn't know how he couldn't feel the way she was burning.

"It lets me do this." He tilted her chin up, so that her throat was exposed, and planted a kiss on her neck. He nibbled his way down her bare shoulders, one of his hands grazing the top of her breast. The barely there stubble on his face gently scratched against her skin. Eliot's beard had always grown in fast—if he didn't shave twice a day, he had a full shadow by early evening. The sensation of his stubble pricking against her skin set her body aflame.

That flame began to grow even deeper, radiating from her core, as his hand slid away from her breasts and found the clasps at the back of her dress.

They hit a roadblock, then, as they both tugged at the clasps, which refused to budge. "How the hell…how did you even get this on?"

"I don't know," she gasped, half laughing, half desperate to feel him against her. "But I'm not the only one who's overdressed for the occasion." She slipped off the jacket of his tuxedo and attended to the belt of his trousers while he unbuttoned his white shirt. Finally, he was naked in front of her, while her own dress was no closer to coming off than it had been before.

"I think…" She hesitated. It was such a beautiful dress.

But that was an ever more beautiful man standing in front of her. "I think you're going to have to rip it," she said, silently dying inside just a tiny bit. But the dress didn't matter. She'd had lots of gorgeous gowns in her life. There was only one Eliot. And she needed to be close to him right now.

"Are you sure?"

Her body was sending more urgent signals now. Seeing him in front of her, a vision of sheer male perfection, was turning the rising want within her into a desperate need. She couldn't wait much longer.

"Yes, please. Get me out of here." Her tone was playful, but she was only half joking. The urge to feel his body against hers was growing with an intensity that would not be denied.

His hands grasped the seam at the side of her dress, and he pulled it apart in one long tear. She cried in relief as the dress crumpled to the floor and he gathered her body to his. She arched her back, her breasts feeling full and heavy as they melted against him.

There was nothing between them now but a few wisps of black lace. He slipped his hand

down to her waist, easing one finger in between
her panties and her skin, finding the sensitive
nub between her legs. She felt her knees turn
to water; if she hadn't had her arms wrapped
around his neck, she might not have been able
to stay standing.

He lifted her in his arms, carrying her like a
bride over a threshold into her bedroom, and laid
her down on the bed. He was hard and ready for
her and quickly took a condom from her nightstand to sheath himself. Her body ached for his.

He eased himself onto the bed, keeping himself raised just above her so that his skin barely
brushed hers. She could feel him against her
thigh, and it was all she could do not to wrap
her legs around him and pull him to her.

"Ready?" he said.

"Yes," she breathed, her voice coming out in
a whisper of need.

He entered her slowly, and she felt a delicious tingle throughout her spine as her body
adjusted, her hips rising to meet his of their
own volition. He bent his lips to hers, covering
her mouth, and she pressed her hands against
the back of his head to keep him there. It was
overwhelming to be so consumed by him, to
feel the fire they'd created grow beyond their
own control.

He moved slowly at first, letting the intensity

build, and then their hips began to sway, finding their own rhythm. Their bodies rocked together faster and faster, performing a dance far more intimate and timeless than the one they'd shared earlier that evening.

They pushed one another back and forth over the brink of ecstasy, her body feeling as though it was melting into his. And still the need within her burned and burned, until, finally, he gave one last powerful thrust and shuddered against her, and she felt herself shatter around him.

For a moment, she was unable to move. Her body felt completely satisfied; she couldn't conceive of moving or of ever wanting to leave this exact spot. He recovered faster, disentangling himself from her and lying on his side next to her. He put an arm around her waist and pulled her to him, cupping his body around hers.

Two weeks left.

She'd tried so hard to focus on the present rather than the ending of their arrangement. She had to keep reminding herself that no matter how delicious, how *right* things with Eliot felt, she couldn't allow herself to want any more than he was offering. Their time together was about writing a new ending to their story, one that didn't involve so much pain. In two weeks, they wouldn't break up. Instead, they would say goodbye to each other. They'd allow each other to move on.

You can't lose something you don't have, she reminded herself.

So why did it feel as though she was about to lose him all over again?

The next morning, Bria woke first. She allowed herself to indulge in a few seconds of gazing at Eliot. As always, his face was so unguarded in sleep, his breathing deep and untroubled, his muscular frame relaxed. It would be a shame to wake him, but they both needed to be up for work soon.

She started their coffee, fixing his just the way he liked it.

Last night had felt surreal. The dress, the ballroom, dancing with Eliot—all of it had felt like something from a fantasy. As terrifying as delivering one of the quints in an elevator had been, when all five babies were born, she and Eliot had shared a moment of triumph. She cast her gaze over the clothes strewn about the floor. The ruined dress.

Worth it, she thought. Sometimes a girl had to sacrifice a great dress for even greater sex. She had no regrets.

Telling off her father had been incredibly satisfying as well. She paused while stirring her coffee, suddenly remembering what her father had said. He'd claimed he knew something about Eliot that she didn't. That everyone owed him something, including Eliot.

She tried to ignore the nagging feeling. Her father was pompous and controlling. Perhaps he simply wanted to *believe* that Eliot owed him something. Or perhaps whatever he'd said was utter nonsense.

The emergency births of the quints had pushed the question out of her mind, but now she found herself mulling over it again. She and Eliot had agreed not to talk about the past. But what if there was something in his past that she needed to know?

Isn't that a little hypocritical? her conscience goaded her.

After six years, there were probably plenty of things she didn't know about Eliot. But there was also something she hadn't told him. She'd never come clean about the real reason she'd broken up with him.

Last night, she'd told her father that there was nothing he could do to hurt Eliot now. But she suddenly realized that was true for her as well. Eliot was no longer a vulnerable young doctor at the start of his career. He had built his fortune independently, and he was successful enough that there was little her father could do to affect his career. Which meant that there was no reason for her not to explain that she had broken up with him under pressure from her father. She'd lied to him, and she'd hurt him deeply to cover up that lie.

She had to tell him the truth, she knew. The past few weeks of sleeping with Eliot had been magical, but whatever she'd tried to tell herself, she knew they hadn't provided the sense of closure that she'd hoped for. After standing up to her father last night, she thought she might know why. After all these years, she finally had a chance to undo the hurt she'd caused Eliot years ago.

They'd agreed not to talk about the past, but she needed to explain this. She needed him to know that she'd only done it to protect him. She hoped it wasn't too much of a reach to think that he might understand and forgive her. Maybe then, when he left to go back to his successful business in Boston, she'd finally have the closure she was looking for.

He shifted in the bed, then stretched and batted his eyes open. She sat beside him and handed him his coffee, which he set on the nightstand so he could pull her close and nuzzle her hair with his nose.

"What's for breakfast?" he murmured.

"Oh, were you going to make us breakfast?"

she teased. "I've got cereal and some eggs in the fridge. Feel free to fix anything you like."

He took little nibbles of her shoulder. "I've already got what I want right here."

For a few moments, there was silence as the subject of breakfast was forgotten. But then he groaned as she disentangled herself from him. "We have to go to work," she said, standing up and heading for the kitchen.

"Just a few more minutes."

"Nope. We can't be late. And there's, um, something I want to talk about with you first." She had to tell him today, she decided. Now that she'd decided to tell Eliot the truth, she wanted the secret to be out as soon as possible.

"What's on your mind?" He was pulling clothes from the small tote bag he'd begun keeping at her apartment. She watched as he slipped into a pair of jeans and then began buttoning a white collared shirt over his chest.

She took a deep breath. "It's about what happened six years ago."

He cocked an eyebrow at her. "Are you sure you want to go there? Every time we talk about the past, we end up fighting."

"I don't think we will this time. Because there's something you don't know. Something I've never been able to tell you, until now."

"Well, now I'm intrigued. What is it?"

She squeezed her eyes shut, then forced them open. She owed it to him to look him in the eye as she told him this. "My father forced me to break up with you. I was never ashamed of you. I never once felt that you weren't good enough for me. I was just afraid of what my father would do to you if we stayed together."

His jaw had formed a firm, hard line that she couldn't read. "What were you afraid he'd do?"

"He threatened to ruin your career. I knew he'd do it, too. Nothing stands in my father's way when he's determined. And I knew that if *you* knew he'd threatened you, that you wouldn't run from him. You'd want to face him. You'd want to prove to him that he couldn't control you. But you didn't know him like I did. I knew that if he wanted to, he'd destroy your career before it even started, and I couldn't let him do that to you."

"So instead you let me believe that you didn't care about me? That you thought I wasn't good enough for you?"

"To protect you," she said weakly.

"To protect me." His voice was cold. Somehow, he didn't seem to be taking this with the relief she'd anticipated.

"I couldn't see any other solution," she tried to explain. "I knew you'd want to fight my father, and I knew he'd win. I'm sorry, but at that time, given who he was and where you were in your life, I knew he'd win. He always did. And he'd have ruined you."

He finished buttoning his shirt and began to put on his shoes.

"Where are you going? Don't you want to wait for breakfast?"

"I don't think so. I think I've had enough for today."

"Why are you so upset?"

"Do you really not understand?"

"No," she whispered. She couldn't imagine how her attempt at honesty had gone wrong so quickly.

"Then maybe I can help you with that. You say you broke up with me to protect me. But you did it by telling me that I wasn't good enough. That I could never make you happy. That we were from two different worlds, and that no matter who I became, my background would never change. You said we'd always be two different people who would want different things. Do you have any idea how that made me feel? After years of being teased and bullied, can you imagine how it felt to hear the woman I loved, that I wanted to marry, say that I wasn't good enough for her? You've got a really strange idea of protection."

"I know it hurt you to hear those things. I

didn't understand how badly until recently. But I only knew that I needed to say something that would throw you off track so you wouldn't think my father was behind it all. Something you'd believe."

His eyes burned into her very soul. "And you knew I'd believe that, because I did grow up poor. You knew that I'd heard I wasn't good enough from people just like you, and you used it against me."

"I had to, Eliot. It was for your sake."

"Is that right? If it was for me, then why did you make the decision yourself, without ever telling me about it? You knew I'd want to stand up to your father, to stand up to him together, and so you decided all by yourself to take that choice away from me."

"Was I wrong, though? Look at all that's happened since. You're a respected doctor *and* a multimillionaire. Could you have done that if my father had been bent on trying to destroy you so early in your career?"

"I'd have found a way to make my life successful. And it would have been my choice. And—" he almost choked on the words "—we could have been together. If you'd trusted me, if you'd had any faith in our relationship, we could have had six years together. But instead of the two of us being a team, you kept this secret and made the decision on your own. Just like you always did with everything else."

Now she was upset, frustrated that he couldn't seem to understand that she was just as upset about the loss of the last six years as he was. It had been a sacrifice that had felt like she'd torn her own heart out, but she'd made that sacrifice for him. Yet he seemed determined to blame her for it.

"You should be the one to talk about secrets," she retorted. "I talked to my father last night, and I know you've got one of your own."

His face blanched, and she realized she'd been hoping that he would deny it. That he'd say her father was just trying to stir up trouble. But she could tell from the look in his eyes that she'd hit on something he didn't want to talk about.

Whether he wanted to talk about it or not, she deserved to hear it. The time for secrets was long past. "What is it, Eliot? Why does my father seem to think you owe him something?"

"Because I do." The expression on his face looked utterly defeated. It was how she felt, too.

"What do you mean?"

"After we broke up, your father offered me a large sum of money to keep quiet about our breakup, and to sign a nondisclosure agreement promising that I wouldn't say anything about your family in the press."

"And you took it?" she asked numbly.

"No! I tore the check up in his face. But then…"

She nodded mechanically. She knew her father well enough. Whatever the details might be, he'd have found a way to force Eliot to take the money.

"He made it impossible for me to refuse."

"How much did he give you?"

"Quite a bit. Enough to pay off my medical school loans and start investing. Two hundred and fifty thousand dollars."

The amount jogged something in her memory. "Then the anonymous donation that came into the Women's Health Center last night?"

"Yes. It was from me."

"Wow. Just wow. So your donation didn't really have anything to do with wanting to support me or the center. It was just some sick, twisted way of paying my father back."

The hurt cut deeper than she'd ever thought it could. The idea that Eliot would use her, and a cause she cared about, to settle some old score with her father was appalling. For the past six years, she'd done everything she could to earn her independence. But now, the night after she'd organized a gala to save her own health center, she learned that her success wasn't about her at all. It was about something her father had done years ago. And it hurt her more than she could say to think that Eliot had been a part of it.

"You don't have to look at it that way," he protested. "The truth is that I can never pay that money back. If I hadn't gotten it at that exact time, I'd have spent the past six years watching my student loans grow larger and larger with interest, instead of paying them off and investing. The fact is that I do owe my entire fortune to your father, and I hate that. You can't imagine how much I hate it."

"How do you think I feel, with you donating the same amount he gave you to the center?"

"It wasn't about him. I wanted to help you. Or is that only all right when you're the one doing all the helping, making all the decisions?"

"Not fair, Eliot. You don't get to hold on to your resentment about the disparity in our incomes when your wealth came from my father all along!"

"You don't understand."

"I understand that you kept a secret from me. One that makes you a total hypocrite. You objected to me keeping something from you when you did the same. And you knew I stepped away from my family's money to get away from my father's control, while you'd taken it all along."

"But that's not how it was. There were extenuating circumstances."

"I'm sure there were. My father's great at finding those. But the point is, you didn't tell me about it. Whatever the circumstances were, you held back from telling me, just like you always do, and left me out in the cold. And I can't do that. I can't keep wondering what's going on with you, what you're thinking and feeling. What you're keeping from me."

"Well, you won't have to wonder too much longer," he said bitterly. "I'll be leaving in two weeks. And not a moment too soon, I'm sure."

She felt as though he'd slapped her. She'd thought there were no longer ways they could hurt each other, but apparently she'd been wrong. "You should go now," she said icily. "We've gotten our closure. We've shared our secrets. If there's anything more to say, I don't need to know. I just need you to leave."

"Gladly," he said. He grabbed his tote bag and stormed out the door.

Funny, she thought as he left. She thought she'd cried all the tears she had over their relationship. But somehow, she'd just managed to find a few more.

CHAPTER NINE

"I HAVE SOME good news."

Caleb seemed to be in a cheerful mood. Eliot raised his head from his hands. After his disastrous morning with Bria, he'd gone home, showered and gone straight to his office. His attempts to start the morning anew had not been successful. He kept hearing the pain in Bria's voice.

Caleb's visit was a welcome distraction from his thoughts. "We've found a doctor to take over as chief of obstetrics," he said. "His name's Dr. Phillips. He's older and very experienced."

"That is good news." Eliot tried to muster some enthusiasm. The hospital had performed an aggressive search for a new chair of obstetrics during his time there, hoping to find someone permanent before he left. St. Raymond's small budget had made the search difficult, as the most talented doctors often went elsewhere for higher pay. They'd been very lucky to have someone as dedicated as Caleb working there for so long, and though he wouldn't say so himself, they'd been just as lucky to have Eliot to replace him.

"Hey, try to look a little excited," Caleb said. "This means that you can return to Boston earlier than expected. You can enjoy some time off, or get back to work and your own life sooner, if you'd like. I thought you'd be glad to hear it." He gave Eliot a sidelong look. "Don't tell me you've changed your mind and decided you want to stay, now that we've finally found someone else to take the job."

"Oh, no. In fact, I think going back early might be a good idea."

"Really? Because the way you and Bria were dancing last night, I thought...that maybe there'd be something to keep you here a little longer. Or someone."

"No," Eliot said brusquely. "Not at all. Bria and I are just friends." His tongue almost tripped over the word *friends*. If there was a less accurate word to describe their relationship, he couldn't think of it.

"I see," said Caleb, giving Eliot a long look. "Then maybe I just misread things."

"Yeah. Well. Easy mistake to make." He knew that Caleb would be willing to listen if he wanted to talk, but he didn't think he could bring himself to discuss Bria. It had been difficult enough getting over her the first time. And now, even though they'd meant to keep things on a physical level, he somehow found himself feeling an overwhelming sense of loss once again. He didn't understand how things had gotten so out of hand, and he didn't think he had it in him to tell anyone else. Even his most trusted friend. He tried to turn the conversation back to business. "I think the sooner I go back to Boston, the better. I've got a lot of work waiting for me there. I'll take a couple of days to help with the transition of the new doctor, and then I'll head home."

"I understand. It's been good to have you for as long as we did."

Two days left in Portland, then. He wondered how he should tell Bria. When she'd agreed to a solely physical relationship, she'd done so on the condition that they'd have a proper goodbye. But that had been before their argument. She'd practically kicked him out of her apartment that morning. Did she even want to see him again?

He'd leave her a note, he decided. That way, he couldn't be accused of breaking his promise. But he'd also be able to avoid seeing the hurt in her eyes again and hearing the accusation in her voice. Accusations that he still didn't think were completely fair considering her own actions six years ago.

He'd be back in Boston before he knew it, and he wouldn't have to worry about her judgment then. And then he could finally go about the business of moving on.

Bria stood up from her desk and stretched. For once, her workday was ending at a reasonable hour. It was just after 5:00 p.m., and she and Hazel had accomplished a long day of administrative chores. As tedious as all those tasks had been, it was also heartening to see that the center's financial situation had improved hugely. At least one thing in her life was going well.

Eliot had been gone for a week. The note that he'd left her lay crumpled at the bottom of her wastepaper basket. It had been brief, and even without looking at it, she recalled perfectly well what it said.

Bria,
I know you wanted us to have a proper goodbye this time, but I'm not sure either of us wants to go through that. Maybe this note can be something in between. I don't have any regrets about our time together, back then or now. But you're right, I did keep a secret from you when I shouldn't have, and I'm sorry for that. I'm sorry we both hurt each other as much as we did.

At least we know now that it just wasn't
meant to be.

Eliot

Upon reading it, she'd immediately crumpled up the paper and thrown it away. What
was wrong with him? How could he leave without any warning, almost two full weeks before
his time in Portland was supposed to be over?
She knew the hospital had found a new doctor, so there was no reason for him to stay at
St. Raymond's. And in fairness, he had no reason to stay for her, either. Not after that terrible
morning together. But she hadn't expected to
say goodbye so soon. And she hadn't expected
that their goodbye would be via a note.

So much for closure, she thought.

Their sex-only, no-emotions-involved fling
was supposed to help her get Eliot out of her
system so she could move on. Instead, she now
found her mind swirling with more questions
than ever.

Why on earth had Eliot had to ruin everything with his stupid pride? Why on earth had
he had to donate two hundred and fifty thousand dollars? Why couldn't it have been two
hundred thousand, or three hundred thousand,
if that amount of money was so easy for him
to give away?

When she'd first learned of Eliot's large fortune, she hadn't ever thought that he could be like her father. She'd trusted that for Eliot, money wasn't about control. But by donating the exact amount of his medical school tuition, Eliot had done the exact thing she'd never wanted anyone to do. He'd taken something she'd built and made it about her father, and about money, too. She'd spent the past six years connecting with the things that felt truly important to her in life, and money hadn't been one of them. But Eliot didn't seem to have learned any lessons from the past. His action proved that he was just as insecure about money as he'd ever been.

The fund-raising gala had been a huge success. But it was a bittersweet victory for Bria. She was glad the center had what it needed—for now—but she knew they wouldn't have reached their goal without Eliot's huge donation.

As upset as she was about his choice, she couldn't help wondering if she'd done the same thing to him. Eliot's furious reaction to her revelation about their breakup and the accusations he'd thrown at her had been so unexpected. And yet, on reflection, she had to admit that he had a point. She'd made a decision for both of them, without even having a conversation about it with him. She'd just assumed that her father would crush Eliot, because she'd seen him crush people before. She hadn't imagined for even one second that Eliot might have triumphed over Calvin Thomas. Where had her faith in her fiancé been?

She hadn't known, back then, that he'd felt as though she made all the decisions in their relationship. But he was right. Back then, that was exactly what she'd done, right up until the breakup. That had been her decision, too. She'd chosen to protect him when she should have confided in him instead. Not only had she told him he wasn't good enough, which had devastated him, but she'd also reinforced that lie by choosing not to trust him with the real story of why she'd felt she had to end things.

And now he was gone, along with any chance of the two of them ever being together.

As much as she'd tried not to let herself want anything more than the physical fling they'd agreed on, she'd been fooling herself all along. She loved Eliot. She'd known the moment she'd seen him again a few weeks ago that her feelings were as strong as they'd ever been. Stronger, in fact, because she'd grown.

Growing up, Bria's life would have looked perfectly charmed to any outside observer. Everyone told her that she was treated like a princess. But she'd never felt like a princess, or special in any way. Until she'd found Eliot.

He'd been the only person in her life who'd ever made her feel that sense of warmth, of rightness, of *family*. Since her mother died, she hadn't had that sense of comfort, and of being at home, until she met him.

That was why it had hurt so much to have it torn away from her. After their first breakup, she'd felt herself drowning, and she'd floundered for a long time before she'd figured out how to save herself.

She'd tried to make a few other relationships work in her dysfunctional love life, but the way she felt after losing Eliot was on a completely different level. There was no one else like him, she knew. Certainly there wouldn't be for her. After losing him twice, she knew that for sure. She still loved him, despite how complicated things had grown between them. She'd probably always love him. But they'd ruined their second chance, and she couldn't see how they would ever have a third.

Thinking of him was as painful as it ever had been. She was looking forward to going for an after-work hike to find some solace in nature. But just as she was about to leave, she thought better of it. One of the quints had been showing signs of labored breathing, and she thought she should run over to St. Raymond's to check on him.

"Are you heading out, too?" asked Hazel, who was also leaving her office.

"I was going to. But I just thought that I should do a quick check on Sandra and the quints."

"Is that necessary? They're in good hands with the staff there."

Bria hesitated. She hated to speak ill of another medical professional, but she had her doubts about Dr. Phillips, the new obstetrician working at St. Raymond's. He was an older man whose résumé contained a long list of previous hospitals he'd worked at. But the more Bria saw of him, the more concerned she became that Dr. Phillips's résumé was so long because he couldn't get along with the staff at those other hospitals. At St. Raymond's, he was short-tempered, dismissive of staff suggestions and had a paternalistic, all-knowing attitude.

Dr. Phillips was a physician with twenty years of experience, and she was only a midwife. Intellectually, she knew she should trust that Dr. Phillips would look after his patients with whatever care was necessary. But her gut instinct told her that something was amiss, though she wasn't sure what it was.

Hazel noted her hesitation. "Dr. Phillips doesn't exactly inspire confidence, does he?"

Bria grimaced. "I know it's not really my

place to challenge how he cares for his patients. But I don't think it would hurt anything to do a few extra check-ins with the quintuplets."

"Tell you what. You look like you're eager for a nice hike. Why don't you go off and enjoy yourself, and I'll run over to St. Raymond's to check on them?"

"Oh, Hazel, you don't have to do that. Especially when there's probably nothing wrong with them—it's just me being paranoid."

"I don't mind. I've had an easy day today— it's no trouble to do one thing more. And between you and me... I have my doubts about Dr. Phillips, too."

"He's only been here a short time."

"That's true. Maybe he'll settle in after a while and everyone will get used to him. But I don't think any of us are thrilled with the first impression he's made."

Bria hated to create more work for her friend, but she was relieved by Hazel's offer. She longed to be in the open air and to have the quiet solace of nature around her.

When she arrived at Forest Park, she opted not to take her usual hike up past the Witch's Castle. Her nerves were far too sensitive to visit a place that held recent memories of Eliot. She swallowed the lump in her throat and headed down another, less frequently used trail. It was a trail that didn't attract nearly as many hikers, which was fine with her. Solitude was what she craved.

She trudged through the woods, the hike somehow not providing the comfort that she'd so often felt in the past. The trees around her were lush and green, their branches bending over the trail to create inviting archways to pass through. The air was completely still except for the occasional rustle of leaves as some small chipmunk or insect hopped about its business. The earthy smell of foliage hung thick around her, and she inhaled deeply, trying to lose herself in the peacefulness of the setting.

She was so lost in thought that she hiked much farther than she meant to. By the time she realized she should be getting home, she was very far down the trail. The sun was setting later these days, but she knew she'd have to move fast if she was going to make it out of the park before sundown.

But as she was trudging back, she came to a fork in the road. She realized she'd been ruminating so much on thoughts of Eliot that she hadn't noticed which direction she'd taken on her hike out. She picked the way she thought she'd come, hurrying even more now, but the road only seemed to take her deeper into the forest.

Frustrated, she decided to turn back again. But now darkness was falling, and it was getting difficult to see.

She passed a large rock that she was absolutely certain she didn't remember and sat down on it, confused.

Where the hell was she?

"Hey, try not to look like you're going to a funeral." One of the firm's senior partners clapped Eliot on the shoulder. "This is great news. You've just graduated from millionaire to billionaire. And let me tell you, you're going to enjoy the difference."

He was back in Boston, sitting in his company's boardroom. They'd called him in to share what they thought would be some good news: they were promoting him to senior partner.

His time away at St. Raymond's had led them all to realize just how badly they needed him, they'd said. They wanted to make sure he realized the vast amount of earning potential he had, not just for the firm, but for himself. That led into yet another discussion of his medical license. The partners were putting even more pressure on him to give it up, once and for all. It wasn't just that his time away had cost the firm money. He was costing himself millions, as well. If he put the time he spent on medicine into the business, he'd eventually retire at an early age with a stock portfolio potentially worth billions.

The partners seemed certain that Eliot wouldn't walk away from such an offer. And honestly, he didn't see how he could. It was so much money. Wasn't that everything he'd wanted? After a childhood of being bullied and teased about his poverty, he'd never feel disrespected again in his life.

He didn't see any reasonable way he could walk away from what they were offering. He'd nodded and listened as they'd spoken, only pausing to ask if it wouldn't be possible to keep his medical license current for the sake of nostalgia. Absolutely not, they'd replied. They didn't want to risk him taking off for any more "medical vacations," as he had at St. Raymond's. Everyone seemed to think that Eliot should be thrilled with this turn of events.

He was trying, very hard, to see it as good news. If he couldn't have a life with Bria, then at least he could have this.

He'd lost her forever, he knew. He'd thought that amassing a fortune of his own would finally give him the security he was looking for. And yes, all his millions had made his life easier in certain ways. But his money still hadn't brought him the happiness he'd been looking for. Even before he'd reconnected with Bria, his love life had been an absolute mess. The women he met all seemed far more interested in his money than in his personality.

But Bria had repeatedly proven to him that she was different. He'd just been too blinded by his own insecurity to see it. It was true that she'd hurt him badly by ending their engagement the way she had. He wished she'd talked to him first. But ultimately he could see now that she'd done it out of love for him. She'd hadn't wanted to break up with him, but she'd sacrificed their relationship so that he could have the career he'd said he wanted.

He might blame her for making that decision without him, but wasn't he just as much to blame? If he'd been more open about what he was feeling back then, would she have been able to put more trust in their relationship, in *him*, and talk to him about what her father was threatening to do? Maybe he could have convinced her that he wouldn't have cared about having to work longer and harder to build a career outside of her father's influence, as long as they had each other. He was no stranger to hard work.

Instead, she'd tried to protect him from her father and from himself. And she hadn't felt she could discuss that decision with him. Even then, she'd known how insecure he was. He'd accused her of using that knowledge against him, but he knew now that he was his own worst enemy. All she'd tried to do was make a sacrifice for his career. A career that he was about to give up, throw away—all for money.

Rich or poor, Bria had shown him what was important to her. Loving someone, and being loved in return, mattered far more to her than what someone had, or how much. He'd been the one who couldn't see that. Who'd let his resentment of their financial disparity come between them.

He didn't deserve her, and he couldn't imagine that she would ever take him back. He knew he loved her. But when you loved someone and failed them, weren't you supposed to let them move on?

He tried very hard to take some pleasure in the opportunity the senior partners were offering him. But his smile didn't come naturally. Supposedly, the partners were handing him everything he'd ever dreamed of, and yet he felt as though someone else were in control, telling him when to smile, when to nod and when to sign on the dotted line.

He went back to his office and rested his head in his hands. He couldn't turn down the offer. He needed to take it. If not for himself, then on behalf of every kid like him who'd ever struggled to fit in as a scholarship student, everyone who'd been told that they'd never make it because they didn't live in the right kind of house or didn't have the background or connections they needed.

But the truth was, he missed St. Raymond's. He missed the pride he'd felt after helping every single newborn into the world. He missed the exhilaration he felt with special cases, especially the quints. They'd been named Joseph, Murphy, Rosemary, Oliver and Sophie. All of them had been doing well when he'd left, although he'd been a little concerned about Oliver's breathing. The new chief of obstetrics had told him not to worry about it, as all premature babies needed extra time for lung development. Still, he hoped someone was keeping a careful eye on Oliver. He was sure Bria would watch over him with extra care. She was such an attentive midwife. If there was anything to worry about, she wouldn't miss it.

But thinking about Bria again only led to wanting her—again. He wished there was some way to shut off his thoughts, but they came rushing into his mind regardless of his wishes. The way his head fit perfectly into the crook of her neck as they lay in bed, the scent of her hair as he buried his nose in it. The heat of her skin as he kissed her neck, the feeling of her moving next to him.

It's over, he thought. *Accept it. Try to think about something else.*

At least at St. Raymond's he'd been able to immerse himself in work that interested him. Here, he had nothing better than stock reports to focus on, and those barely held his attention.

Suddenly, he sat straight up in his chair. The quintuplets. Baby Oliver's wheezing. He knew what was wrong.

His hand hovered over his phone, ready to call St. Raymond's. He hesitated. Surely the new doctor would catch anything amiss. But at that thought, his unease grew. He hadn't been impressed with Dr. Phillips and had only grudgingly relinquished his patients to the man's care because he hadn't seen that there was any other option. He wasn't sure that Dr. Phillips would make the right diagnosis. And he might take umbrage at Eliot's interference, since Eliot was no longer the attending physician.

But this was no time for professional niceties. Eliot dialed St. Raymond's and asked to be connected to the NICU.

"I need to speak with Dr. Phillips immediately," he said. "It's a matter of some urgency about one of the quintuplets."

Hazel had answered the phone. "I'm sorry, Eliot, but that won't be possible."

"It's an emergency, Hazel."

"I understand, but Dr. Phillips is no longer here. He was fired and left immediately. He really wasn't able to get along with any of the staff, and then he and Dr. Anderson had quite the falling-out."

Fired? So St. Raymond's was without a chief of obstetrics again? He pushed the thought from his mind; that wasn't important now. "Look, it doesn't matter. Baby Oliver needs to be tested immediately for respiratory syncytial virus."

"Oh my god. You suspect RSV?"

"I didn't at first. I attributed his trouble breathing to underdeveloped lungs, just as Dr. Phillips did. But the more I thought about it…"

"No, you're right. The wheezing, the fast breathing, the way his nose and chest look…it all fits. I'll get him tested immediately. Thank you, Eliot. I'm so glad you called."

So was he. Even if he'd lost Bria forever, the phone call had given him clarity about one thing: he was a doctor.

The knowledge hit him in the gut, the same way he'd made baby Oliver's diagnosis. No matter how much money someone offered him to do something else, he would always be a doctor. And there was no denying it. He'd tried

for years, and he'd ended up right back here—
on the phone, saving a patient and knowing he
would never quit.

The partners would be perfectly fine running
the company without him. He didn't need more
money. But there was a hospital in Portland that
needed him now. Even if Bria didn't want him,
that hospital was where he belonged. He might
not be able to be with her, but at least he finally
knew who he was. If he couldn't have her, then
that would have to be enough.

He opened his mouth to ask Hazel if he could
talk to the chief of staff, but before he could
speak, Hazel said, "Eliot, I think you should
know something."

"What is it?" Her tone made him apprehensive.

"It's Bria. She's…she's in bad shape."

His heart suddenly felt very full. Was she
struggling just as much as he was? Was Bria
there? Could he talk to her? There was so much
he wanted to say. "I know," he said gently. "But
I'd really like to speak with her, if she's willing."

"You can't," said Hazel. His heart plummeted.
What else were you expecting? he admonished
himself. *It's over, she doesn't want you.*

He'd thought Hazel would hang up, but she
continued, her voice tearful. "She's been injured. She's here, in the ICU. She's been here

for a few days. I don't know if she would want me to tell you or not. I couldn't ask her, because she's..." Hazel paused and seemed to fight for composure. "She's in and out of consciousness. But I thought you should know." Hazel hung up. Eliot stared at the phone, frozen.

Bria was in the ICU?

His mind swam with questions. From the sound of things, her condition was very serious. *Don't panic—it won't help.* He could almost hear Bria's voice saying the words. He knew that if she were here, the first thing she'd do would be to try to get him to calm down.

But she wasn't here. She was in a hospital bed, thousands of miles away, and he had no idea what had happened or how to help.

Half a second ago, he'd thought he'd finally gotten his life figured out when he realized he needed to go back to Portland to be a doctor. But now it seemed that everything was wrong. Bria being injured was wrong. Him being in Boston was wrong.

Everything was wrong, and he wasn't sure how to fix any of it.

But he had an idea about where to start.

CHAPTER TEN

BRIA FADED IN and out of consciousness. She was dimly aware of having been brought to the ICU, but it seemed as though her memory was playing tricks on her. She wasn't entirely certain of what was real. She thought she remembered the concerned face of a park ranger, an ambulance ride and then doctors speaking over her in urgent, quiet tones. But at other times she felt as though she was still in the forest, waiting for someone to find her.

She'd gotten lost in the woods. It had been getting dark, and she was starting to grow concerned about just how deep she'd traveled into the park without paying much attention to her surroundings. Her phone wasn't getting any reception at all, and her maps application simply showed her as deep in the woods somewhere, with no clear instructions as to how to get out. The compass kept reorienting itself in different directions.

She'd finally found a rock that she could sit on comfortably, but when she did, she'd been so frustrated and so tired that she'd made a rookie hiking mistake: she'd put her hand on the ground behind her to steady herself without looking to see what was there first.

She'd heard an unearthly rattle, and before she could move, there was instant pain. Whatever had bitten her disappeared in an instant, but the two small, bloody dots on her hand only began to look more serious as time went on. Within five minutes, her hand felt as though it was burning.

She'd never heard a rattlesnake's rattle, except perhaps in films, but there had been no mistaking that sound. She'd earned her first-ever snakebite, and at the worst possible time. She was lost in the woods, and it was growing dark.

Snake venom, she knew, traveled not through the blood but through the lymphatic system. As long as she didn't move, the venom wouldn't travel through her tissue fluid. In theory, she could lie here indefinitely. Assuming she didn't die of exposure first. Or another snakebite. Or starvation.

Stop that. It's a popular hiking trail in a public park. Someone will come along eventually.

Yes, eventually, but how long would that take? And it was a huge public park, with long, winding hiking trails. She'd chosen one of the less popular trails specifically because she'd wanted to be alone. And night was coming on fast.

The pain in her hand made it hard to keep still. She wanted nothing more than to cradle it to her chest and curl up in pain. Instead, it took everything she had to remain flat on her back, willing herself not to move.

Her strategy wasn't going to work, she realized as the minutes ticked away. For one thing, she couldn't keep her hand completely still. The pain was so bad that her hand jerked every few minutes, and it was impossible to keep her face an expressionless mask—fear and pain led her to gasp and cry out. She couldn't stay completely motionless for the amount of time it would take for someone to find her. She needed to try something else.

She stood up. She'd give herself three minutes, she decided, to walk briskly in the direction of a trailhead. Any trailhead. It didn't matter whether it was back the way she'd come. She just needed to get to a place where other hikers were more likely to walk by. Or where she could get a phone signal. A phone signal would be even better.

She headed down one of the trails, keeping an eye on her phone in case the reception bars sprang up. When three minutes had passed, she'd come close to a fork in the road. Hopefully close enough that someone would see her when they passed by. Her entire arm was on fire now; she didn't dare walk any more. She lay flat on her back again. As she did, she noticed that her phone had one tiny reception bar that flickered in and out.

Her strength was rapidly ebbing as she dialed the emergency number with her good hand. After that, her memories became less reliable.

Sometimes it seemed as though she could hear Hazel's voice calling to her. At other times, it felt as though she was still lying on her back in the woods, listening to the rustle of the leaves and wondering whether the noises she heard were caused by people or wild animals. Sometimes it seemed as though she could hear Eliot's voice, but that made the least sense of all, because Eliot was gone. She'd lost him forever, because she hadn't seen that she could trust him after all.

She could make out voices every time her mind roused itself, but it was difficult to stay focused on them. She heard little snatches of conversations. Everyone sounded so worried, and she tried to let them know that they didn't need to be. But every time she spoke, someone told her to rest.

People kept telling her that she was brave,

that she was showing so much courage. She didn't have the strength to tell them they were wrong. All she was doing was lying in a bed, while other people drew blood and gave injections, doing their best to save her life. All she could do was trust them.

Thinking about trust brought her back to Eliot again. She'd always told him he needed to be less guarded, more open, but had she proven herself to be the kind of person he could open up to? She didn't think so.

And now, even if she survived this ordeal, she'd be just as alone as ever. She knew she was drifting in and out of consciousness, but part of her didn't even want to fight to stay awake. Eliot still wouldn't be there, and it was hard to think about waking up without him.

She'd been so naive to think that she could ever agree to a meaningless fling with him with zero consequences. Eliot was the love of her life. That would always be true, even if she never saw him again.

She heard Hazel speaking with two doctors. One of them did sound like Eliot, but she was dimly aware that she was probably delirious and that her mind was likely to fabricate things.

"Her arm's swelled to twice its normal size," she heard one of them say. "There's a serious risk of compartment syndrome."

"Isn't there anything you can do?" That was the doctor who sounded like Eliot.

"She's already had more than twenty vials of antivenin. If we'd gotten to her any later, she would have died. She'll be very lucky if we can save her arm."

"Whose arm are you talking about?" she wanted to say, but when she heard her voice come out, it only sounded like a dull moan. They couldn't be talking about her arm. She was a midwife; her hands and arms were her tools. How many babies had she cradled with her own arms? Maybe one hundred? She needed her arms to work.

"We should have this conversation some-where else."

"I don't want to leave her," said the Eliot-sounding doctor. Now she knew it definitely couldn't be him. She'd ruined her second chance with him, and there wouldn't be any more. Eliot wouldn't say he didn't want to leave her, be-cause he was already gone.

"I understand, but she might be able to hear us, and I don't want her disturbed. The best thing we can all do right now is let her rest."

Three days later, Bria blinked her eyes open. She could see now that she was, indeed, in an ICU. She'd had some sense of it while she was delirious, but she hadn't been sure. There was a heart rate monitor next to her, and her right arm was splinted and completely wrapped in bandages.

But the most surprising sight of all was Eliot, sitting in a chair across from her bed.

There were dark circles under his eyes, but she could still see the light buried within their brown depths as they gazed at her with warm concern. He looked as though he hadn't slept in days. His face was worn and haggard, his hair askew, and his stubble almost grown into a beard. He'd never looked better to her.

But why was he here?

"Hey," she croaked, her voice dry from disuse. "Aren't you supposed to be in Boston?"

"Don't worry about that right now. Here, have some water." She sipped from the straw he held for her, grateful to feel the coolness on her parched throat. But her curiosity about what he was doing by her bedside was too great to ignore.

"You're the one who looks worried," she said, her voice coming out more clearly now that she'd had something to drink. "What are you doing here? Why did you come back?"

He hung his head, almost as though he was afraid to meet her eyes. But then he did look up at her, and his eyes were warm and full of contrition. "Because from almost the minute my plane landed back in Boston, I realized I'd done something incredibly stupid. I wasn't where I needed to be. I'd left people who were depending on me. And…" He reached across Bria and took hold of her good hand. "I made a mistake that almost cost me the most important person in my life."

The warmth of his hand felt so good against hers. She noticed tears in his eyes, and she felt tears forming at the corners of hers, as well. And then a tear did fall down his cheek. She moved to wipe it away, but he said, "Don't. The doctors want you to move as little as possible."

"But I don't want you to be sad," she said.

"I know," he said. "I should have known that a long time ago. You've only ever wanted me to be happy."

She leaned back into the hospital bed. Despite her low energy, she was fighting a strong desire to leap up and throw her arms around him. She longed to tell him everything she'd realized over the past few days, about how unfair she'd been and how much she regretted that she'd wasted their second chance. But she'd also just been delirious, and she had no idea for how long. She was still trying to convince herself that he really was here, in the flesh.

"You're really here?" she asked him.

"I'm really here. And I'm not going anywhere."

But what about his job in Boston? Clearly, there were a few gaps in her understanding of recent events. "Um, Eliot? Could you catch me up a little on what's happened?"

"Well, first of all, it's been a week since you came in."

"A *week*?" Bria sat up in alarm.

"No sudden movements, or you'll get me kicked out of your room and Hazel will bite my head off."

She relaxed. Now that Eliot was here, she didn't want anything to send him away. Even a well-meaning best friend. "A whole week?" she said, shaking her head. How could she have lost that much time without realizing it?

Suddenly, she remembered something important. Something about the way one of the quintuplets had been breathing had raised a red flag in the back of her mind; she'd meant to keep an eye on it. "Eliot—how have the quintuplets been doing? I wanted to keep Oliver closely monitored."

"Oliver is fine."

"But—"

"Bria." His hand over hers was firm. "Will you please let me take care of you first before we start talking about patients?"

"Sorry," said Bria, mollified. "Please continue."

"You were brought in and treated for a real beauty of a rattlesnake bite. You were out for about seven days, during which time your arm just kept getting bigger and bigger. Everyone was scared that you might have compartment syndrome. There was some pretty serious talk of amputation."

So she hadn't imagined that part. Bria shivered.

"I'm not trying to scare you, I'm just trying to explain why *we* were all very scared over the past few days, and why I want you to take it easy. But the good news is that as long as you are very careful and follow the doctor's orders to the exact letter, you should be able to keep your arm." He raised an eyebrow in warning. "And I'll be watching to make sure that you take very good care of yourself."

"Because you're not going anywhere."

"That is indeed what I said. I'm glad you're keeping up."

"Okay. I want to know exactly *why* you aren't going anywhere. But first, Oliver. Has Dr. Phillips looked at him? Is he going to be all right?"

"Oliver is fine. He was tested for RSV. We were able to start treatment extremely early, and his prognosis is looking good. As for Dr. Phillips, he is no longer at St. Raymond's, due to being incompetent and unable to get along with anyone. But that's all right, because the hospital has a new chief of obstetrics."

"Who?"

"Me."

"Then you chose medicine!" she said, relieved. She'd known he was born to be a doctor, and she knew it brought him joy he couldn't get in another profession, no matter how much money he made.

"I did." Eliot smiled. "I got the partners in Boston to buy me out. I'm a doctor full-time now. All I have is my meager salary, a fulfilling profession...and a fortune in the bank. I think I'll be all right."

"And you really are staying in Portland!"

He shook his head. "As we've now established for the third time, I'm not going anywhere. But I hope you don't think that's because of a job."

"It's not?"

"No. Not at all. I can get a job anywhere. That's not why I'm staying in Portland."

She'd thought that might be the case, but she couldn't quite let herself believe it. A torturous, agonizing hope was rising in her chest.

She'd ruined everything. She'd spoiled their time together, and she hadn't trusted in him or in their relationship. She'd been just as closed off as she was always accusing him of being.

And yet he was here. He'd said she was the most important person in his life. And apparently, he wasn't going anywhere.

"But *why* aren't you going anywhere?"

"I'm working up to that part," he said softly.

"Does it need working up to?"

"It does. Because, you see, I thought you might die." The tears were coming back into his eyes again.

"Hey," she said. "How come I'm the one who suffered a snakebite but you're the one who looks like they've been run over by a truck?"

"Because I thought I'd lost you."

She smiled, trying to reassure him. "Well, guess what? I'm not going anywhere, either."

"I'm glad to hear it. Because when someone you love almost dies, it helps you to realize a few things."

The agonizing hope that had been rising within her began to soothe itself. It was turning into a warm glow. It was no longer the kind of hope that tortured. Instead, it was the kind of hope that breathed life into her. All because of that little four-letter word he'd uttered. It was going to be hard to concentrate on anything else he had to say, because that word kept looming larger in her mind. He loved her.

"Bria, I have to tell you something."

She smiled. "I think you might have already told me the most important part."

"Which is?"

"That you love me."

"But I have to tell you all the other things first. I have to apologize for being a fool, and for not understanding that you were trying to help me when I needed it. For doubting you when you had the best of intentions. For not seeing you for who you really are. I let my own past get the better of me, and it cost us…*us*. And even though I know it's unlikely, I came here hoping against all hope that you might consider giving me another chance. Because I love you, Bria Thomas. You make me feel alive, and I promise you that if you let me love you again, this time I'll never let you go."

She squeezed his hand. "What about my apologies? I made so many mistakes, too. I lied to you about wanting to break up, and I didn't trust you when you needed me to. I didn't trust you when you could have helped both of us. I could have confided in you, but instead I just made a huge decision on my own. One that cost us six years of happiness."

"You can make those apologies if you need to. But I don't need to hear them. Because I know how I feel about you, and frankly, I'm much more interested in hearing how you feel about me. And about the idea of the two of us, together."

"I think it's the best idea I've heard in six years," she said. "Because I love you, too. I never stopped. You're the one I want to spend the rest of my life with, and you always have been."

He kissed her then, a soft, sensuous kiss that was full of promise. She smiled a bit as she inhaled the faint scent of cinnamon on him. There were so many ways in which they'd both changed, and yet the best parts of him had always been there, waiting to be seen.

As they broke apart, she said, "I promise that from now on, I'll make sure I'm not making unilateral decisions, but that I'm including you and that we're working as a team."

"And I'll tell you what's going on with me rather than hiding my feelings and keeping you shut out in the cold."

"Wow," she said. "Call me crazy, but I think we might actually have the makings of a mature, adult relationship."

"Maybe even more than that," he said. "I was thinking that we just made something that sounded like vows to one another."

Her heart soared. "I was thinking that, too."

"In that case…" He took her uninjured hand

in both of his and got down on one knee. "Bria Thomas—"

"Yes," she laughed before he could finish.

"Really?" he said. "For richer or poorer?"

"I think that has to be a given with the two of us."

He leaned in and kissed her. She could tell he meant to be gentle, but she wasn't. She put every last ounce of love she had for him into it, every bit of energy she could spare to let him know exactly how loved he was. She'd spent the past few days fretting over all the chances in life and in love that she hadn't taken. From now on, she planned to make the most of every moment, starting with this kiss.

EPILOGUE

One year later

THE EARLY FALL leaves made a satisfying crunch under Bria's feet. The air was crisp but still warm enough for a Saturday morning picnic near the open-air market. The tradition that Bria and Hazel shared had evolved over the past few months. Now she and Eliot spent their mornings at the market with Hazel, Caleb and Caleb's nineteen-year-old daughter, Lizzie, and sometimes they were joined by Lizzie's fiancé, Derek. Each weekend, they would all split up to find something to eat from a different booth— perhaps some local honey, a new kind of cheese or a loaf of artisan bread. When they returned, they made a picnic out of their findings. It was quickly becoming one of Bria's favorite Saturday rituals.

This morning, she and Eliot were the first to return to the agreed-upon spot by the river. Bria had brought an old wool blanket once owned by her mother to spread upon the ground, and she snuggled into Eliot's arms as they sat on the riverbank, watching people make their way into the market.

"It's nice to have a moment to ourselves," he said, his arm around her, his nose nuzzling into her hair. "I thought being married meant we'd have *more* time to spend together, but I feel like I haven't seen you in days."

"That's your fault for being such an important doctor," she replied, leaning back to kiss him. Over the past year, word of the quintuplets' birth had spread within the medical community, and St. Raymond's was becoming even more well-known as a hospital that specialized in complicated pregnancies. Eliot now spent his days immersed in hospital work, and Bria could tell that he loved every minute of it.

"I've been working too much, haven't I?" he said, his face drawn with concern. "We could have had a more elaborate wedding if I'd taken more time off."

"Nonsense," she said, putting a hand on his arm. "Our wedding was perfect." After Bria's recovery, they'd both wanted to get married as quickly as possible, and so the ceremony had been a tiny affair, nothing more than a small gathering of their closest friends at city hall.

Eliot's mother had flown in from Aruba; she'd welcomed Bria with open arms and made her feel like family.

"Perfectly efficient. I can't imagine it was the wedding of your dreams."

She nudged him playfully. "Now you're just trying to get me to say it."

"To say what?" he said, his eyes wide and innocent.

"To say that any wedding to you would be the wedding of my dreams." She leaned back to kiss him again.

"You're right," he said. "I have to admit that I do enjoy hearing you say that."

"Ahem!" Lizzie had arrived with a loaf of bread. "Are we here to have a picnic or engage in PDA?"

"Sorry, Lizzie," Bria said, motioning for the girl to sit down beside them. "We'll try to keep the public displays of affection to a minimum."

"But no promises," Eliot said wryly, wrapping his arms tightly around Bria's waist.

Lizzie rolled her eyes as she sat next to Bria and dropped her loaf of bread onto the blanket. "I can't believe you haven't gone on your honeymoon yet. When Derek and I get married, we want to take a grand tour of Europe, starting with Paris, and then hit all the romantic spots in Italy. Well, that's what we'd do if we had loads of cash, anyway. How can the two of you stay here when you've got millions in the bank?"

"Lizzie!" Caleb had just arrived over the knoll. "Don't be rude."

"It's all right." Bria smiled. "Everyone has a different idea of what makes them happy. For us, happiness means being here with our friends."

"It's kind of you to say that, but I know you've delayed your trip for Hazel," Caleb said. That had indeed been a strong practical reason to delay the honeymoon, as Bria refused to leave the country before Hazel gave birth. She was overdue now and very ready to meet her baby.

"There couldn't be a better reason for us to stay," she told Caleb. And she meant it. There couldn't have been a better reason to delay the honeymoon…except, perhaps, for the additional information she and Eliot had received last night. But she'd need to wait for Hazel to arrive before she revealed that particular piece of news.

"Where is Hazel, anyway?" asked Lizzie, echoing Bria's thoughts. "I'd have thought she'd be back by now."

"Me, too," said Caleb. His expression was worried, as it always was these days whenever Hazel left his side for more than five minutes. Bria knew that Caleb's first wife had died due to a pulmonary embolism after an emergency cesarean section, and she understood Caleb's anxious hovering. She could even relate to it, to a degree. Even though Bria had assured Caleb throughout the pregnancy that Hazel was doing wonderfully, she'd been absolutely determined to be Hazel's midwife. She knew that Hazel would be in excellent hands no matter who assisted with the delivery, but she still felt more comfortable with the idea of overseeing things herself. It must be hard for Caleb, she thought, to focus on being a husband rather than an obstetrician.

Just as she was wondering if she should text Hazel to check on her, everyone's cell phone began to whirr at once. As Bria opened her phone, she saw a group text from Hazel: BABY911.

A moment later, a second whirring followed up the first: CHEESE STALL.

After a stunned moment, Bria felt her brain snap back into action. "Caleb," she said. He was staring at the phone in shock. "Caleb?"

"I can't believe I left her alone," he gasped. "She wanted us each to go to different stalls, like always. I should have said no. She's all alone and it's my fault."

"Caleb!" Bria almost shouted, using her most authoritative voice. "She's not alone, she's got us. That's why she texted. Where are your car keys?"

"My keys?"

"Give them to Lizzie, right now." Bria turned to Lizzie. "You're going to be our driver. Run and get your dad's car and park at the bottom of the hill. We'll meet you there as soon as we can."

Unless things progress a lot faster than expected.

A glance at Eliot's face told her he was thinking the same thing.

But if it came to that, she was ready. One baby in a cheese stall couldn't be that difficult compared to some of the other situations she'd encountered. At least she wasn't facing quintuplets in an elevator.

"Don't worry," she said to Caleb, infusing as much confidence as she could into her voice as they hurried down the hill toward the market. "We'll have her at the Women's Health Center in no time. You'll be celebrating the birth of your second child before you know it."

Caleb nodded at her, but the look of dread on his face didn't change.

They did, in fact, make it to the Women's Health Center in time, thanks to some bold driving on Lizzie's part. Hazel was glad to see Caleb become noticeably less distressed once they finally had Hazel set up in one of the birthing rooms, though the worry never completely left his eyes.

"You're both doing wonderfully," Bria said. Caleb held Hazel's hand as she breathed steadily.

"How much longer?" gasped Hazel.

"Not long at all now," Bria reassured her. "You're fully dilated."

Both Hazel and Caleb grew tense. "Then why—" they both began at once.

Bria cut them off. "The labor's progressing, but more slowly than it should. That's not surprising, given that the baby's in breech position."

Hazel lay back and groaned.

"She needs a cesarean," Caleb said. "We should get her to St. Raymond's immediately."

"Hold on," said Bria gently. How true it was that doctors made the worst patients. Caleb was ready to jump into action at the exact moment she needed both him and Hazel to calm down and take things slowly.

But that, she supposed, was why they had a midwife on hand. Bria was determined not to let her best friend down.

"No one's going anywhere until you start breathing again, just like we've practiced," she said to Hazel in her firmest tones. To her relief, Hazel began her deep breaths again. Caleb, however, still looked recalcitrant.

"She needs to be in a hospital. In case something goes wrong, in case we need to act quickly…"

Bria knew that the loss of his first wife had to be weighing heavily on Caleb's mind. But that was nearly twenty years ago now. He was wrapped up in his fear from the past, and she needed him to be with her today, right now, with her and Hazel.

"Caleb," she said gently, "look at Hazel. Look at how well she's breathing. I want you to squeeze her hand." He did as Hazel smiled up at him.

"We're going to get through this together, but we need to go *slowly*. Can you do that?"

Caleb looked at Hazel. "It's your call," he said.

"I want our baby to be born here," she replied. She nodded at Bria. "I'm ready."

Bria smiled. "Good, because so is baby." As Hazel had resumed breathing, the baby's hindquarters had slowly been making their way into the world. Bria gently eased the baby along with each of Hazel's contractions until the baby's legs were out.

She'd known the baby's sex for months, but Hazel and Caleb had wanted to be surprised. She gave them both a wink. "Just a few moments more and the big secret's out. Ready, Hazel?"

Hazel gasped and nodded, and Bria rotated the baby until she could feel the cheekbones with her fingers. "One more big push," she said to Hazel, and with the next contraction, a slippery bundle shot into her arms.

Caleb was still shaking with relief, so Bria opted to hand the tiny bundle to Hazel. "Would you like a few moments to yourselves?" she asked as Hazel and Caleb gazed down into the brand-new pair of eyes before them.

"No," said Hazel. Tears streamed down her face as she tore her gaze from the baby and looked up at Bria. "I want everyone here. Lizzie should be part of this, and you and Eliot, too."

"Agreed," said Caleb. "Joy is better when it's shared, and we…" His voice choked. "We have a lot to share."

"I'll go get them." Bria stepped into the hall, where Eliot and Lizzie had been waiting. "Well?" Lizzie cried as she rushed in. "Do I finally get to know whether I have a baby sister or brother?"

"It's a boy," said Caleb, barely able to contain his pride.

Hazel beamed up at him. "We've got our little Darcy."

Bria felt Eliot's arm around her waist. As

happy as she was for Hazel, she didn't resist as he pulled her back into the hallway. After the intensity of the birth, it was a relief to feel his arms around her, sturdy and reassuring.

He pulled her close and murmured into her ear. "Think we'll be that happy when our turn comes around?"

"Shh! They'll hear you. I don't want to intrude on the moment with our big announcement."

Eliot glanced into the birthing room, where all eyes were fixated on baby Darcy. "I have a feeling you don't need to worry about them overhearing us for now." He put a hand on Bria's stomach. "Still, you should probably give Hazel a little warning that you'll be needing her services as a midwife in a few months."

Bria twined her arms around Eliot's neck and leaned up on tiptoe to kiss him. "I'll be sure to let her know well before the time comes. We'll let them celebrate today and share our own joy tomorrow."

Eliot's arms grew tighter around her waist. "I never knew," he said, gazing into her eyes. He seemed about to say more, but his lips bent to kiss her first.

As much as Bria was interested to know what he had to say, she found she was quite unable to pull herself away from his kiss, and so quite some time passed before she was able to say, "You never knew what?"

"Hmm?"

"You said, 'I never knew,' and then we got a bit distracted."

"Ah. Yes. I was going to say that I never knew how much there could be to celebrate in life. So much, in fact, that for the first time in my life, I feel…rich."

Her heart burst with love for him. She knew exactly what he meant. After all the years they'd lost waiting for each other, after all the times they'd nearly missed finding each other again, it was hard to believe that there could be so much joy in their lives. The new life growing within her was a miracle in more ways than one. They were indeed rich, with so much to be thankful for.

"We both are," she said, tears brimming her eyes. "In all the ways that count."

He gave a sigh of deep contentment. "Shall we head back in there?"

"In just a moment," she said, pulling his head toward hers again. Just like Eliot, she'd never known, never even dreamed, that she would have so much joy in her life. And now that she did, she wasn't going to let it go.

* * * * *